BASS

Power Crystal

Once a Star Darling has granted her first wish and returns to Starland, she receives a very special treasure—a beautiful Power Crystal.

BELT

Wish Pendant

A Wish Pendant is a powerful accessory worn by a Star Darling. On Wishworld, it helps her identify her Wisher and store the ever-important wish energy.

Instrument

Each girl in the Star Darlings band has a unique musical talent that helps her light up the stage.

Vega and the Fashion Disaster

NPL F

Nashville Public Library   FOUNDATION

*This book given
to the Nashville Public Library
through the generosity of the*
**Dollar General
Literacy Foundation**

NPLF.ORG

Vega and the Fashion Disaster

Shana Muldoon Zappa and Ahmet Zappa

with Zelda Rose

𝔇𝒾𝓈𝓃𝑒𝔂 Press

Los Angeles • New York

Printed in the United States of America
Reinforced Binding
First Paperback Edition, January 2016
1 3 5 7 9 10 8 6 4 2

FAC-029261-15324

Library of Congress Control Number: 2015946377
ISBN 978-1-4847-1306-8

SUSTAINABLE FORESTRY INITIATIVE

Certified Chain of Custody
Promoting Sustainable Forestry

www.sfiprogram.org
SFI-01054

The SFI label applies to the text stock

For more Disney Press fun, visit www.disneybooks.com

To our beautiful, sweet treasure,
Halo Violetta Zappa. You are pure light and joy
and our greatest inspiration. We love you soooo much.

May every step upon your path be blessed with positivity and
the understanding that you have the power within you to
manifest the most fulfilling life you can possibly imagine and
more. May you always remember that being different and true
to your highest self makes your inner star shine brighter.

Remember that you have the power of choice. . . . Choose thoughts
that feel good. Choose love and friendship that feed your spirit.
Choose actions for peace and nourishment. Choose boundaries
for the same. Choose what speaks to your creativity and unique
inner voice . . . what truly makes you happy. And always know
that no matter what you choose, you are unconditionally loved.

Look up to the stars and know you are never alone.
When in doubt, go within . . . the answers are all there.
Smiles light the world and laughter is the best medicine.
And NEVER EVER stop making wishes. . . .

Glow for it. . . .
Mommy and Daddy

And to everyone else here on "Wishworld":

May you realize that no matter where you are in life, no
matter what you look like or where you were born, you, too,
have the power within you to create the life of your dreams.
Through celebrating your own uniqueness, thinking positively,
and taking action, you can make your wishes come true.

Smile. The Star Darlings have your back.
We know how startastic you truly are.

Glow for it. . . .
Your friends,
Shana and Ahmet

Student Reports

NAME: Clover
BRIGHT DAY: January 5
FAVORITE COLOR: Purple
INTERESTS: Music, painting, studying
WISH: To be the best songwriter and DJ on Starland
WHY CHOSEN: Clover has great self-discipline, patience, and willpower. She is creative, responsible, dependable, and extremely loyal.
WATCH OUT FOR: Clover can be hard to read and she is reserved with those she doesn't know. She's afraid to take risks and can be a wisecracker at times.
SCHOOL YEAR: Second
POWER CRYSTAL: Panthera
WISH PENDANT: Barrette

NAME: Adora
BRIGHT DAY: February 14
FAVORITE COLOR: Sky blue
INTERESTS: Science, thinking about the future and how she can make it better
WISH: To be the top fashion designer on Starland
WHY CHOSEN: Adora is clever and popular and cares about the world around her. She's a deep thinker.
WATCH OUT FOR: Adora can have her head in the clouds and be thinking about other things.
SCHOOL YEAR: Third
POWER CRYSTAL: Azurica
WISH PENDANT: Watch

NAME: Piper
BRIGHT DAY: March 4
FAVORITE COLOR: Seafoam green
INTERESTS: Composing poetry and writing in her dream journal
WISH: To become the best version of herself she can possibly be and to share that by writing books
WHY CHOSEN: Piper is giving, kind, and sensitive. She is very intuitive and aware.
WATCH OUT FOR: Piper can be dreamy, absentminded, and wishy-washy. She can also be moody and easily swayed by the opinions of others.
SCHOOL YEAR: Second
POWER CRYSTAL: Dreamalite
WISH PENDANT: Bracelets

Starling Academy

NAME: Astra
BRIGHT DAY: April 9
FAVORITE COLOR: Red
INTERESTS: Individual sports
WISH: To be the best athlete on Starland—to win!
WHY CHOSEN: Astra is energetic, brave, clever, and confident. She has boundless energy and is always direct and to the point.
WATCH OUT FOR: Astra is sometimes cocky, self-centered, condescending, and brash.
SCHOOL YEAR: Second
POWER CRYSTAL: Quarrelite
WISH PENDANT: Wristbands

* * * ⭑ * * ⭑ * * ⭑ * *

NAME: Tessa
BRIGHT DAY: May 18
FAVORITE COLOR: Emerald green
INTERESTS: Food, flowers, love
WISH: To be successful enough that she can enjoy a life of luxury
WHY CHOSEN: Tessa is warm, charming, affectionate, trustworthy, and dependable. She has incredible drive and commitment.
WATCH OUT FOR: Tessa does not like to be rushed. She can be quite stubborn and often says no. She does not deal well with change and is prone to exaggeration. She can be easily sidetracked.
SCHOOL YEAR: Third
POWER CRYSTAL: Gossamer
WISH PENDANT: Brooch

* * * ⭑ * * ⭑ * * ⭑ * *

NAME: Gemma
BRIGHT DAY: June 2
FAVORITE COLOR: Orange
INTERESTS: Sharing her thoughts about almost anything
WISH: To be valued for her opinions on everything
WHY CHOSEN: Gemma is friendly, easygoing, funny, extroverted, and social. She knows a little bit about everything.
WATCH OUT FOR: Gemma talks—a lot—and can be a little too honest sometimes and offend others. She can have a short attention span and can be superficial.
SCHOOL YEAR: First
POWER CRYSTAL: Scatterite
WISH PENDANT: Earrings

Student Reports

NAME: Cassie
BRIGHT DAY: July 6
FAVORITE COLOR: White
INTERESTS: Reading, crafting
WISH: To be more independent and confident and less fearful
WHY CHOSEN: Cassie is extremely imaginative and artistic. She is a voracious reader and is loyal, caring, and a good friend. She is very intuitive.
WATCH OUT FOR: Cassie can be distrustful, jealous, moody, and brooding.
SCHOOL YEAR: First
POWER CRYSTAL: Lunalite
WISH PENDANT: Glasses

NAME: Leona
BRIGHT DAY: August 16
FAVORITE COLOR: Gold
INTERESTS: Acting, performing, dressing up
WISH: To be the most famous pop star on Starland
WHY CHOSEN: Leona is confident, hardworking, generous, open-minded, optimistic, caring, and a strong leader.
WATCH OUT FOR: Leona can be vain, opinionated, selfish, bossy, dramatic, and stubborn and is prone to losing her temper.
SCHOOL YEAR: Third
POWER CRYSTAL: Glisten paw
WISH PENDANT: Cuff

NAME: Vega
BRIGHT DAY: September 1
FAVORITE COLOR: Blue
INTERESTS: Exercising, analyzing, cleaning, solving puzzles
WISH: To be the top student at Starling Academy
WHY CHOSEN: Vega is reliable, observant, organized, and very focused.
WATCH OUT FOR: Vega can be opinionated about everything, and she can be fussy, uptight, critical, arrogant, and easily embarrassed.
SCHOOL YEAR: Second
POWER CRYSTAL: Queezle
WISH PENDANT: Belt

Starling Academy

NAME: Libby
BRIGHT DAY: October 12
FAVORITE COLOR: Pink
INTERESTS: Helping others, interior design, art, dancing
WISH: To give everyone what they need—both on Starland and through wish granting on Wishworld
WHY CHOSEN: Libby is generous, articulate, gracious, diplomatic, and kind.
WATCH OUT FOR: Libby can be indecisive and may try too hard to please everyone.
SCHOOL YEAR: First
POWER CRYSTAL: Charmelite
WISH PENDANT: Necklace

NAME: Scarlet
BRIGHT DAY: November 3
FAVORITE COLOR: Black
INTERESTS: Crystal climbing (and other extreme sports), magic, thrill seeking
WISH: To live on Wishworld
WHY CHOSEN: Scarlet is confident, intense, passionate, magnetic, curious, and very brave.
WATCH OUT FOR: Scarlet is a loner and can alienate others by being secretive, arrogant, stubborn, and jealous.
SCHOOL YEAR: Third
POWER CRYSTAL: Ravenstone
WISH PENDANT: Boots

NAME: Sage
BRIGHT DAY: December 1
FAVORITE COLOR: Lavender
INTERESTS: Travel, adventure, telling stories, nature, and philosophy
WISH: To become the best Wish-Granter Starland has ever seen
WHY CHOSEN: Sage is honest, adventurous, curious, optimistic, friendly, and relaxed.
WATCH OUT FOR: Sage has a quick temper! She can also be restless, irresponsible, and too trusting of others' opinions. She may jump to conclusions.
SCHOOL YEAR: First
POWER CRYSTAL: Lavenderite
WISH PENDANT: Necklace

Introduction

You take a deep breath, about to blow out the candles on your birthday cake. Clutching a coin in your fist, you get ready to toss it into the dancing waters of a fountain. You stare at your little brother as you each hold an end of a dried wishbone, about to pull. But what do you do first?

You make a wish, of course!

Ever wonder what happens right after you make that wish? *Not much*, you may be thinking.

Well, you'd be wrong.

Because something quite unexpected happens next. Each and every wish that is made becomes a glowing Wish Orb, invisible to the human eye. This undetectable orb zips through the air and into the heavens, on a one-way trip to the brightest star in the sky—a magnificent place called Starland. Starland is inhabited by Starlings, who look a lot like you and me, except they have a sparkly glow to their skin, and glittery hair in unique colors. And they have one more thing: magical powers. The Starlings use these powers to make good wishes come true, for when good wishes are granted, it results in positive energy. And the Starlings of Starland need this energy to keep their world running.

In case you are wondering, there are three kinds of Wish Orbs:

1) GOOD WISH ORBS. These wishes are positive and helpful and come from the heart. They are pretty and sparkly and are nurtured in climate-controlled Wish-Houses. They bloom into fantastical glowing orbs. When the time is right, they are presented to the appropriate Starling for wish fulfillment.

2) BAD WISH ORBS. These are for selfish, mean-spirited, or negative things. They don't sparkle

at all. They are immediately transported to a special containment center, as they are very dangerous and must not be granted.

3) IMPOSSIBLE WISH ORBS. These wishes are for things, like world peace and disease cures, that simply can't be granted by Starlings. These sparkle with an almost impossibly bright light and are taken to a special area of the Wish-House with tinted windows to contain the glare they produce. The hope is that one day they can be turned into good wishes the Starlings can help grant.

Starlings take their wish granting very seriously. There is a special school, called Starling Academy, that accepts only the best and brightest young Starling girls. They study hard for four years, and when they graduate, they are ready to start traveling to Wishworld to help grant wishes. For as long as anyone can remember, only graduates of wish-granting schools have ever been allowed to travel to Wishworld. But things have changed in a very big way.

Read on for the rest of the story. . . .

ACROSS:

3. Student who went on second mission and identified the wrong wish at first.

5. 4-Down was replaced by another student, named _____.

7. Student who went on first mission and identified wrong Wisher at first.

9. Headmistress of Starling Academy. She came up with the secret plan to send twelve students to Wishworld to collect wish energy.

10. There were band tryouts, and a machine called the _____ chose the members. It also named the band the Star Darlings. That made 9-Across very upset, as it gave up our secret name.

DOWN:

1. This mean student wanted to be lead singer of the band, but she lost. I don't think we've heard the end of it.

2. The head of admissions. She stutters when nervous and trips a lot. Everyone feels a little sorry for her.

4. It was determined that this student's assignment as a Star Darling was a mistake, and she was replaced.

6. All the Star Darlings who have tasted this Wishworld drink love it.

8. Student who went on third mission. Her Wish Pendant was mysteriously ruined. She also did not collect any wish energy.

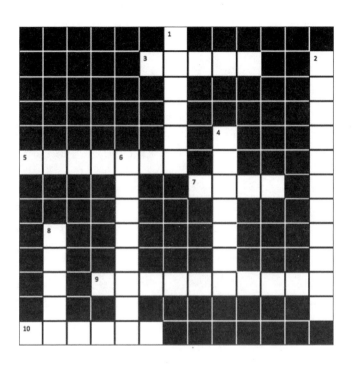

CHAPTER
1

Vega sat on her neatly made bed, staring at the holo–crossword puzzle projected into the air above her Star-Zap. With two flicks of her wrist, she switched the position of two answers, then frowned and returned them to their original places. She nodded, finally satisfied. It was perfect. Vega loved creating puzzles almost as much as she enjoyed solving them. She appreciated crosswords, riddles, puzzles, brainteasers, mazes, and games—anything that challenged her and made her think in a fun and interesting way.

With another flick of her wrist, she erased all the answers, leaving the clues and a blank grid, ready to be filled in. She took a look at her handiwork and sighed.

The real joy in creating a puzzle was sharing it with someone. She wished she could send it to her best friend from home, Enna, who loved games just as much as she. The two girls had even made up a secret holo-alphabet they had both memorized so they could communicate privately. What looked like gibberish to their classmates back at Kaleidoscope Falls Elementary might be a complex message about after-school plans or the guest list for Enna's upcoming Bright Day party.

Sure, Vega belonged to Starling Academy's Puzzle Club, which met after school every Dododay and was filled with like-minded students. It was the first club she had joined since arriving at the school two years before. But the secret nature of the Star Darlings made this crossword something she could not share with anyone except them. So there were only eleven girls she could share it with, and unfortunately, none of them were particularly interested in brainteasers. In fact, they seemed to think Vega's obsession was a little weird. It had been just a starweek or two earlier that she and Leona had found themselves sitting across from each other at lunchtime in the Celestial Café. After they had ordered their meals from the hovering Bot-Bot waiter, Vega had turned to Leona excitedly and said, "Let's guess whose food will arrive first!" and Leona had just laughed.

"Everything is a game to you, Vega, isn't it?" she said. Vega had blinked at her in surprise. It was—and why not? Games made life more interesting. She didn't get why the other girls didn't understand that. Not that she wasn't serious-minded—quite the contrary: she was as focused on her studies as a Starling could be. But she could make studying into a game, too.

As she recalled the conversation, Vega realized that was one of the last times she had heard Leona laugh. Leona's Wish Mission had been a terrible disappointment. (See 8-Down.) Although she had successfully granted her Wisher's wish, Leona's Wish Pendant had malfunctioned, and when she had returned to Starland, she had discovered it was blackened and burnt-looking. As a result, Leona hadn't collected a single drop of wish energy. The usually vivacious girl had been sad and withdrawn ever since. Lady Stella had done her best to convince her it wasn't her fault, but Leona was set on blaming herself.

Lady Stella told everyone to keep attending class (including their special Star Darlings–only class at the end of each school day), learning their lessons, and going on their Wish Missions as planned. The headmistress would be working with some leading wish energy scientists and some trusted faculty members to figure out what had gone wrong with Leona's Wish Pendant and how to fix it. Hopefully they would figure it out soon.

Vega's bass guitar was in its cerulean case, leaning in the corner of the exceptionally neat bedroom. She imagined that it was looking at her reproachfully, as the Star Darlings band hadn't had a rehearsal in a week because of their lead singer's absence during her Wish Mission. They had one scheduled for that day. Would Leona show up? Vega certainly hoped so. They were already down one member due to Scarlet's ouster from the Star Darlings (see 4-Down), and Vega feared that the additional loss of their lead singer could mean the end of the group.

Vega glanced down at her Star-Zap. It was nearly time for practice, and she realized she wanted to be on her way there before her roommate got back from Meditation Club. Vega's strong desire to vacate the premises surprised her. She stood up quickly and smoothed the blue coverlet, which was unnecessary, as its edges were pulled so tightly you could bounce a wharfle on it. She knew because she had tried. Vega's roommate, Piper, kept her side of the room just as neat as Vega's, and Vega counted her lucky stars every day for that. But that's where the similarity ended. Piper's side was dreamy and ethereal, with a gently undulating water bed covered with the softest of linens and more pillows than you could count, the largest embroidered with the word *dream*. Her star-painted dresser contained more nightgowns and pajamas than regular clothes; Vega was sure of it. She had not seen her roommate wear the same thing twice to bed.

Vega stole a quick glance at the mirror hanging on her closet door. Neatly bobbed blue hair, smooth and shiny. Electric blue jacket, sparkly tunic, leggings, and soft ankle boots. She was crisp, polished, and neat as a pin, as usual. She grabbed her bass and turned to head out of the room. The door slid open. Too late.

Piper stood in the doorway, blinking at Vega in her usual sleepy fashion. Her seafoam green hair rippled down her back, past her waist. Her long dress billowed around her feet. She was tall and slender, and whenever Vega looked at her, she couldn't help thinking of a graceful, flowing waterfall.

"Hey," said Vega.

"Hello there," said Piper languidly. She smiled slowly and sighed contentedly. "Meditation Club was starmendously relaxing today." She swiveled her head around and shrugged a couple of times. "I feel like a wet noddle-noodle, like I could just collapse in a heap."

"Maybe you need a nap," Vega suggested starcastically.

Piper's light green eyes lit up. "What a great idea!"

she said. She sauntered to her side of the room and reached for one of the week's worth of sleeping masks that hung from the wall on pretty pegs before kicking off her slippers, pulling on the mask, and curling up on her chaise lounge. She arranged a loosely knit pale green blanket over her. Within arm's reach of her lounge were a basket of holo-diaries for jotting down dreams and a large bouquet of glittery coral-colored flowers, which perfumed the room with an almost magical fragrance. Piper inhaled deeply. "*Mmmmmmm*," she said sleepily.

Vega tried as hard as she could not to roll her eyes at her roommate. Not that Piper could see from under the sleeping mask anyway. Who needed to take an after-meditation nap? Wasn't that redundant? But then she immediately felt bad. From day one it had been quite obvious that ethereal Piper and practical Vega were complete opposites. Vega was direct and serious, and she liked rules. Piper was emotional, otherworldly, and unhurried. But they quickly learned that they had a common love of order and that they often saw situations from two very different angles, which gave them a multidimensional view on many issues.

Soon they developed a grudging admiration for each other. It was a struggle sometimes, but they had made it work. But then, as Vega recalled, things had changed dramatically. They had gone to bed planning a hike to the Crystal Mountains, debating what to bring for lunch, and had woken up the next morning scowling at each other. Piper had started relaying the previous night's dream, which apparently had featured Vega in a starring (and not very flattering) role, and Vega had just cut her off. Now relations between the two were chilly, though usually polite. She could tell it pained the sensitive Piper, and it wasn't pleasant for Vega, either. But there didn't seem to be anything they could do to fix it.

Piper raised her eye mask and looked at Vega. "Are you going to band rehearsal?" she asked.

"You're a regular detective," Vega heard herself say, an edge to her voice as she held up her guitar case. Piper gave a thin-lipped smile and pulled the mask back over her eyes.

Immediately feeling guilty for her rudeness, Vega quickly opened the sliding door, walked out, closed it, and stepped onto the dorm's Cosmic Transporter, a moving sidewalk that ran through it.

Unbeknownst to each other, once they were alone, the two girls gave simultaneous sighs of relief.

CHAPTER
2

"No, no, no, no, no," said Leona, stamping her foot so hard her golden earrings jangled. "You've got it all wrong. All wrong!" She dug her hands into her halo of golden curly hair in frustration.

Vega bit her lip, beginning to wish she had skipped rehearsal. From the looks on her fellow band members' faces, she suspected they felt the same way.

Leona turned to the band's lead guitarist. "Sage," she said. "You're playing too slow. This is rehearsal for a rock band, not an End of the Cycle of Life procession, for stars' sake."

Before the girl could respond, Leona turned to Libby. "And *you're* coming in too soon on the keytar," she scolded.

Libby sucked in her cheeks and stared down at the keys on her portable keyboard.

Vega held her breath, hoping she would be spared Leona's wrath. No such luck. Leona spun around and stared at her for a minute before she spoke.

"And, Vega, you were in the wrong key." She leaned her face close to Vega's. "Don't do that again," she concluded.

Vega felt her cheeks turn red. She generally appreciated Leona's big personality and even occasionally found her dramatic outbursts somewhat entertaining, but that day she felt the girl was just being a big bully.

She watched as Libby took a deep breath, closed her eyes, wiped the frown off her face, and opened her eyes. "Leona," Libby said kindly, "do you need a break?"

This only served to infuriate Leona further. "I don't need a break!" she screeched. "I need a new band."

Clover, who had reluctantly agreed to sub for Scarlet when she hadn't shown up for the last rehearsal, raised her drumsticks and hit the cymbal with a loud crash. She stood up. "That's it," she said. "Guess what, Leona? I don't need to take this. I'm just doing this as a favor. And now I'm out of here." She shoved her drumsticks into her back pocket and stormed off.

Leona spun around, throwing her hands into the air.

"Great, guys, just great," she said. "Now we're drummer-less again. And she wasn't even the problem. It's the three of you!"

Libby, Sage, and Vega glanced at each other. Nobody seemed to be in any rush to argue with the enraged diva. Finally, Libby spoke up. "Leona," she said, putting her hand on the girl's arm. "We understand that you're under a lot of stress right now. But you also have to see things from our point of view. We're learning new songs and we're trying hard and you need to be patient with us. Nobody is going to want to be in your band if you yell all the time. And I don't think you want us to quit, do you?"

Vega was impressed. Libby always could see both sides of a situation and lay them out clearly in a nonjudgmental way. And Leona actually seemed to be listening to her.

"Yeah," Vega added. "You'd have to have tryouts all over again. What if Vivica comes back?"

Vivica was Leona's biggest rival and was still angry that Leona had beaten her to be lead singer of the group. Starting over would be completely unacceptable. Leona's shoulders sagged. "You're right," she said. "I'm just so upset about everything and I guess I'm taking it out on you guys. . . ." Her voice trailed off.

"Of course you're upset," Sage said in a calming

tone. "Listen, it's all going to be okay. We're a good group! Don't forget that we were the ones who were picked out of all the students who tried out. Maybe we should just hold off on practicing until you're feeling better about . . ." Vega noticed that Sage's eyes had lit on the empty spot on Leona's wrist where her Wish Pendant used to be. Once you noticed that, it was almost impossible to look anywhere else. Vega forced herself to stare at Leona's face. "Um, everything that happened," Sage concluded.

"Okay," said Leona softly. She gazed at the ground, unable to look anyone in the eye. "I'll let you know when I'm feeling more up to it." She smiled sadly. "I'm sorry."

The three girls watched as Leona headed toward the Big Dipper Dorm, the slightly bigger and fancier dorm where all the third and fourth years lived.

Vega turned to the two other girls. "Wow," she said. "Do you think she's ever going to get over what happened?"

"She had better," said Sage, "or she's going to lose all her friends. If she hasn't already." She shrugged. "Well, see you later. I have plans to meet some friends and listen to music at the Lightning Lounge." She turned and hurried off.

"What do you think?" Vega asked Libby. But the

pink-haired girl was holo-texting and held up a finger for Vega to hold her thought. Vega did.

"So what do you think about that?" Vega repeated when Libby was finished.

"What do I think? I think we'd better find Scarlet if we want to keep this band together," said Libby. "As much as she and Leona didn't get along, Leona usually behaved around her. And Clover was mad. I don't think she's coming back."

"So no one has seen Scarlet since . . . that day?" Vega asked.

"Well, Tessa told me that Scarlet stopped showing up for their Astronomics class," said Libby. "It's totally bizarre. Nobody's seen her. And nobody knows where her new dorm room is—or even if she has one." She shook her head. "It's a mystery."

Libby's Star-Zap pinged, telling her she had a holo-text. She read it, smiled, and put her guitar back in its pink case, then snapped the case closed. "Adora's at the Serenity Gardens," she reported, "so I'm going to paddle out there and hang out with her until dinnertime. Want to join me?" Vega declined, even though she enjoyed the gardens, a chain of star-shaped islands connected by footbridges that sat in the middle of Luminous Lake. Lush and beautiful, it was a wild place with towering trees, shady nooks, blossoming shrubs, creeping vines, and more varieties of flowers than you could count. The air smelled tantalizingly delicious. But there was a place she liked even better.

"See you at dinner, then," said Libby, walking off toward Luminous Lake. Vega knew she'd grab a hover-canoe at the boathouse on Shimmering Shores. Vega slung her own guitar case over her shoulder and headed to the hedge maze, her favorite spot in all of Starling Academy. The trickily curving paths, which led, eventually, to a lovely seating area in the middle, were surrounded on either side by tall green hedges, so you couldn't see over to the next turn. But this maze was special. Its paths were constantly shifting, so it had limitless possibilities. You never went the same way twice. It was quite challenging. This was delightful to Vega but entirely frustrating and confusing to most of the other students, so Vega knew she would have her privacy. An escape route had recently been added, after a first year had unwisely gone into the hedge maze without her Star-Zap and, unable to find her way out, had to sleep under a hedge overnight. Now a single red florafierce could be found blooming in each wall of the maze. All you had to do was pick it and the maze would immediately form a doorway out. But Vega would never consider using it. Finding her way in an ever-changing maze was too much fun.

Vega could feel all the frustrations of the day magically lift as she stepped between the leafy maze walls. She loved the way the thick hedges towered over her head and framed the blue sky above. She was convinced she did her best thinking as she wandered through its pathways.

She switched on her Star-Zap's holo-video and began recording. She liked to take holo-vids of her day and review them before she got into bed for the night. After she made the first turn, she had a choice of going left or right. Without hesitation, she took the left path. Turning, and turning, and turning some more, she meandered through until she found herself in the center of the maze, which that day featured a display of lallabelle flowers, formed into a star shape, of course. Nearby was a pretty little swing hung with creeping zeldablooms, fragrant and lush. She sat on it and swung back and forth, the slight breeze ruffling her short hair.

Vega opened her guitar case, lifted the blue embroidered strap over her neck, and began to strum, practicing her scales, starting with C major. Her fingers alternated over the frets as she picked out a sequence of notes. Practicing her scales soothed and calmed her, which was good, because Leona's outburst during band practice was still bothering her. It wasn't only that the girl had berated her fellow band members (Vega did not appreciate being yelled at for no good reason), but also that the usually confident Starling was feeling so downtrodden. Plus, she wondered, if they could even find Scarlet, could they convince her to return to the band? Not if Leona was acting like this; that was for sure. Vega thought there must be something she could do to help. Her fingers playing the notes, she swung back and forth, lost in thought. *That's it! I'll holo-text Cassie!* Cassie had struck up an unlikely but warm friendship with Leona. Unlikely because Cassie was as reserved and shy as Leona was loud and confident. But their opposite-personality friendship worked. Vega felt a twinge of remorse. It was just like how she and Piper used to balance each other out.

She reached into her pocket and pulled out her Star-Zap. I'M IN THE HEDGE MAZE. DO YOU HAVE A MINUTE TO TALK ABOUT LEONA? she holo-texted.

The response was immediate: I'LL BE THERE IN TEN STARMINS.

So Vega continued to play, lost in her thoughts about Leona, Scarlet, and Piper. Glancing at her Star-Zap, which sat nearby, she realized the ten starmins were almost up. She put her bass back in its case and began making her way toward the maze entrance. Then her Star-Zap beeped and flashed a small icon of her mother's face. It was in a red star, a reminder that she had not yet returned her mother's holo-call from two stardays earlier. Vega considered doing it right then and there, but she still wasn't ready. She knew her mom was going to ask her to come home for a visit (again), and Vega needed to come up with a reason that she couldn't (again). She had already used a fellow student's Bright Day celebration she couldn't miss, a Glowin' Glions game, and an extra-credit assignment. She was running out of excuses. Vega felt uneasy. She wasn't exactly sure when things between her and her mom had gotten so complicated, but she figured it must have been around the time the two had seemed to switch roles. Vega had reached the Age of Fulfillment and overnight, it seemed, had transformed from a carefree child to an über-responsible, grades-obsessed perfectionist. She was determined to get into Starling Academy at any cost and had focused all her energy on studying. (She took the entrance examination five times to get the rare perfect score, which she was sure would guarantee her acceptance. Luckily, she loved tests, seeing them as the ultimate game.) And perhaps because her mother, Virginia, realized she no longer needed to worry about her daughter, she changed from a constantly stressed-out single mom into a relaxed, fun-loving person. The two rarely saw eye to eye on anything these days, so Vega alternately missed her mom terribly and was relieved by the distance between them.

Vega turned a corner and spotted Cassie, who looked flustered. She had somehow gotten turned around and was headed the wrong way.

"Hey, Cassie," Vega called.

Cassie spun around, a frown on her pale, pretty face. She was wearing a white diaphanous baby-doll dress shot through with silver thread over a pair of calf-length white leggings and a white tank top. She had delicate silver sandals on her feet.

"Oh, there you are," Cassie said, sounding faintly put out. She blinked up at Vega through her star-shaped glasses, her silvery hair done up in her signature pigtail buns. Vega smiled at the girl.

"Stop it," Cassie snapped.

"Stop what?" Vega asked innocently.

"You're looking at me like I'm some precious little doll," Cassie replied. "You know how much I hate that."

"Sorry," said Vega with an embarrassed grin. She couldn't help it. It was true. Cassie was so tiny and cute, even when she was scowling.

"Well, thank goodness I found you," said Cassie. "You know how this maze drives me crazy."

Vega opened her mouth, about to mention that it was actually *she* who had found Cassie. But the irritated look on Cassie's face told her to keep that thought to herself.

"I'm glad you holo-texted me," Cassie said as the two girls made their way back to the hedge entrance.

They reached a place where they could turn either right or left. Cassie started to go to the right and Vega tapped her on the shoulder. "This way," Vega said, pointing in the opposite direction.

Cassie shrugged. "Whatever you say. You're the expert." She glanced at Vega. "So was Scarlet at practice today?"

Vega shook her head.

Cassie looked disappointed. "So weird," she said. "No one's seen her since that awful day. . . ." Her voice trailed off.

Vega winced, recalling the fear in the pit of her stomach when they all realized Lady Stella was going to tell one of them that she was about to be ousted from the Star Darlings. After all her hard work, it would have been such a blow to her. She had actually frozen with terror at the thought. But as she had looked around the room, she'd realized that each of the eleven other girls felt the same way.

Cassie looked at the ground. "I still feel guilty over how happy I was that it wasn't me," she said.

Vega nodded. "I think we all do."

A sly smile crossed Cassie's face. "Everyone except Leona," she said. "I think she was glad to see Scarlet go." The smile quickly left. "But now Leona's got her own troubles." She looked up at Vega. "Is that what you wanted to talk about?"

Vega took a deep breath. "It's just that Leona's not herself," she said. She filled Cassie in on that afternoon's outburst.

"Oh, that's bad," said Cassie, biting her lip. "She loves the band. That's such a shame."

Vega put her hands to her forehead. "We should be able to help her get through this. Get everything back to normal. But I have no idea how. That's where you come in. You two are such good friends." The thought of losing the band was very upsetting to Vega. She took everything seriously—her classes, her studies, the meals she ate (to give her energy), the time she went to bed (so she'd be well rested for the next day's classes). Even her beloved games—she was a stickler for following the rules. When she played her bass, it was the only time she ever really let loose and relaxed. She did not want to give that up.

Cassie grimaced. "We *used* to be good friends," she said. "But she's been keeping to herself lately. The only person she seems to want to spend time with these star-days is her new roommate, Ophelia." She thought for a moment, then nodded as if she had made up her mind. "I'm going to try to talk to Leona after dinner," she said. "Will you come with me?"

"Sure," said Vega, shrugging.

Cassie's mood brightened considerably. Vega thought that it was probably both because they had a plan and because they were approaching the end of the maze. Cassie breathed a sigh of relief as they walked out the leafy doorway. The Celestial Café came into sight, and Vega's stomach rumbled at the same time that the large star above the door began to blink, letting every-one know that it was dinnertime. Perfect. The two girls headed to the building. Inside the large, warmly lit room, soft music was playing. There was the soothing sound of students softly chattering and the clink of silverware against fine china. They headed to the table that had unofficially become the Star Darlings', with its stun-ning view of the Crystal Mountains. To the rest of the school, they were a group of girls—four first years, four second years, and four third years—who attended regular classes but required some extra help during last period. Only the Star Darlings; Lady Stella, the headmistress; Lady Cordial, the head of admissions; and a handful of professors knew who they really were. Vega found that some students treated her differently (a small number of those scornfully, though many were sympathetic), while most didn't seem to care that she was "different." Little did they know that Vega and her fellow Star Darlings were really special in the very best way. That didn't matter to Vega, who didn't really care what others thought of her. It was enough for her to be singled out as special by someone she had admired for a long time: Lady Stella. In the hopes that she would one day be chosen to attend Starling Academy, Vega had devoured every holo-article that had been written about the headmistress.

There were three empty seats at the table, and Cassie and Vega sat next to each other. They missed out on the seats facing the radiant Crystal Mountains, but the light of the setting sun hit the mountain peaks, refracting into stunning mini rainbows that bounced off the shining goblets and illuminated everyone's face.

"So how was Wish Theory class today, Adora?" Vega asked as she unfolded her soft cloth napkin and laid it on her lap. The Star Darlings always made certain to limit their conversations to non–Star Darlings business when they were in eye- and earshot of the rest of the student body. They had been warned countless times that the work they were doing was top secret. Even most of the faculty had no idea what was going on.

"A snore," said Adora with a rueful grin. Professor Illumia Wickes liked to let her students run the class discussions, which was oftentimes wonderful, unless you had an incessant talker in the class. "This girl named Moonaria would not stop talking. No one could get a word in edgewise."

Vega nodded in sympathy. She watched as Tessa entered the cafeteria and, seeing that the only free seat was next to her roommate, Adora, leaned over and whispered in her sister's ear. Gemma rolled her eyes and moved into that seat, leaving the seat next to Leona open for Tessa. Vega noticed that Cassie was openly staring at Leona, who kept leaning over to whisper in Ophelia's ear. Leona was being unusually quiet, and the rest of the girls stole glances at her, as well, used to being entertained by the girl at mealtimes. She would often lead the girls in a sing-along or start a game of holo-telephone. Once the message had started off as "Glow for it! You are starmendous!" But by the time it got to the end of the line, it had been completely mangled, and poor Cassie had squeaked out, "You've got it! Glowfurs are delicious!" and everyone roared with laughter. Cassie had seemed way more humiliated than she should have been about her mistake, in Vega's opinion. But she had not been able to figure out why.

Astra leaned over. "Why so quiet, Leona?"

Leona simply shook her head. Her expression clearly read *Leave me alone*. Astra looked like she was going to try again, but Cassie elbowed her in the ribs.

"Ouch," said Astra, rubbing her side. She and Leona both had very big personalities. The two usually enjoyed a friendly rivalry, which occasionally resulted in the butting of heads and angry words. But they rarely stayed mad at each other for long. Astra looked confused.

Finally, Cassie leaned over and whispered in Astra's ear. Vega wasn't sure what she had said, but she thought she could guess the gist of it: *Leave Leona alone; she's fragile*. Astra looked disappointed. Whether it was that she felt sorry for Leona or missed her sparring partner, Vega was not sure.

The look on Cassie's face as she watched Leona from across the table was also impossible to decipher—jealous, wistful, or maybe just curious. Next Vega studied Ophelia, who was smiling shyly, her orange-pigtailed head bent to the side to listen to Leona's whispered comments. She seemed like a very nice, quiet girl, and Vega found herself wishing that *she* was the Star Darling who had been assigned the new roommate instead of Leona. The fact that Piper would have to have been expelled from the Star Darlings for that to happen did not escape her, and she silently chided herself for her unkind thoughts.

Vega found her appetite was not diminished by the strange goings-on and polished off her garble-greens soufflé and moon cheese popovers. After the Bot-Bot waiters had cleared the table, she ordered a mug of piping hot Zing and a cocomoon pavlova. The food at Starling Academy was top-notch, and although she wasn't quite as into food as Tessa (who hadn't been able to decide between two desserts, so had ordered both), she appreciated eating well—especially after many nights of popping a premade Sparkle Meal into the oven when her mother was on the overnight shift at the hospital. As a nurse, her hours were long and she couldn't miss a day unless it was an absolute emergency. Vega had learned at a young age what constituted an emergency: not much. She sighed, remembering the many nights she had eaten alone at the kitchen table while doing her homework.

She looked around and smiled. Maybe that's why she felt so fierce about being a Star Darling and keeping everyone together and happy. It was nice to be part of a group, to literally have a place at the table among friends.

After polishing off the last bite of her dessert, Vega swigged the rest of her Zing and stood, pushing her chair back from the table. She was ready to march over to Leona, and she turned to ask Cassie to join her. Cassie grabbed her arm. "Let's wait a minute," she said softly, "and see where Ophelia goes. I'd like to talk to Leona alone." They discreetly followed the two Star Darlings out of the cafeteria. Sure enough, once outside, the two girls parted ways.

After a moment, Leona noticed their presence and gave them a wan smile. "Hello, girls," she said.

Cassie leaned forward for a closer look at Leona. "Did you take your sparkle shower today?" she asked in a concerned voice. Vega blinked, suddenly realizing that Leona's skin was not quite as glittery as usual. She once again wished she was as observant as Cassie, who never seemed to miss a detail. All Starlings had a shimmery glow, and they supplemented it with daily bathing in a shower of weightless sparkles. It was a great way to start the day, as it revitalized and invigorated you, improving your mood and outlook and also refreshing your spar-kle. Some Starlings took them twice a day, but Vega felt that was a bit excessive and a daily shower was perfect. It was funny: Leona, with her golden hair, coloring, and clothing, always managed to look extra glittery. But not that night.

"Of course," said Leona. Then she paused and wrinkled her brow, thinking about it. "I mean, I think so. Maybe," she concluded.

Cassie gave Vega a despairing look. Leona was usu-ally vain about her appearance. This was so unlike her.

The Cosmic Transporter dropped them off between the two dorms. The first and second years lived in the Little Dipper Dorm, and the third and fourth years lived in the Big Dipper Dorm. Cassie clearly wanted Leona to invite them to her room, but the girl was not cooperat-ing. She looked at them quizzically as they shifted their feet. "Well, I'll see you la—" Leona started.

"Hey, mind if we drop by?" Cassie interrupted. "I haven't been over in a while."

Leona shrugged halfheartedly. "Sure," she said.

They walked through the doors and stepped onto the Cosmic Transporter that looped its way through the large dormitory, dropping students off in front of their doors. They headed to her room in a silence that seemed awkward to Vega. She and Cassie weren't used to having to carry a conversation when Leona was around. The transporter deposited the three in front of Leona's door, and she placed her hand on the scanner. The simple gesture seemed to take considerable effort. "Welcome, Leona," the soothing Bot-Bot voice said, and the scanner glowed bright blue as the door slid open. The girls stepped inside behind her.

"It's a little messy," Leona said awkwardly. "I've been kind of, um, busy lately."

A little! That was the understatement of the star-century. Vega was shocked by the state of the room. Offices, dorm rooms, public spaces, houses, classrooms, restaurants, stores—every space on Starland—were self-cleaning. Scrubbing, scouring, mopping, sweeping, vacuuming, and washing were unheard of on Starland, which was why Wishling tools such as mops, brooms, pails, cleansers, sponges, and, most of all, the frighteningly loud contraptions Wishlings called vacuums completely confused Starlings. But Starlings weren't entirely off the hook when it came to cleanliness: they still had to hang their clothes, place their holo-books on the shelves, and throw their garbage into the vanishing garbage cans. Leona had clearly not tidied up in a while. Vega shuddered with distaste as she took in the clothing draped over chairs, the burned-out lightbulb in Leona's three-sided vanity mirror, the pile of jujufruit peels on the floor. Her large round pedestal bed was unmade. Gliony, Leona's stuffed talking lion who never said the same affirmation twice, sat forlornly on the floor, on his head. Cassie picked him up and righted him. "Shine on, bright Starling," he said. Cassie placed him on Leona's shelf and patted his mane.

Vega looked around the room. Leona's stage, a golden star-shaped platform used for her daily performance, was littered with star-shaped stuffed creatures, pillows, and holo-magazines. The disco ball, which usually spun, filling the room with dancing stars of light, was turned off. The trunk she used to store her glamorous golden costumes was empty, its contents strewn about on the floor. The sheer messiness of Leona's side made the contrast with the other side of the room even more shocking. Leona's untidy half was giving Vega a headache, but she was shocked to see that Ophelia didn't seem to have anything *to* organize. Her side was just . . . sad. There was a plain solar-metal bed with a simple white moonfeather comforter. The tiny chest of drawers made it clear she didn't have a lot of clothing, either.

The lone spot of color on Ophelia's side of the room was a thin orange ribbon that trimmed her plain white bedding.

"Your roommate doesn't have a lot of belongings, does she?" Vega observed.

"No, she doesn't," said Leona with a hint of defensiveness. "She likes to keep things simple."

"Not a holo-book or a holo-photo?" Cassie pressed. "Not a single stuffed creature?" It was clear she was trying to keep her tone light, but Vega could see that Leona was starting to bristle at the questions. To Vega's surprise, the usually sensitive Cassie plowed on. She picked up a tiny crystal that sat on Ophelia's dresser and placed it in her palm. It was a miniature version of the beautiful crystal her own roommate, Sage, displayed in their dorm room, which she had received as a Bright Day gift.

"So tiny!" she marveled. "More like a chip than an actual crystal . . ."

"Put that down!" Leona snapped.

Cassie's eyes widened and she set it back on the dresser like it was burning her hand. She stared down at her silver slippers, looking like she might cry. Then she seemed to gather herself, taking a deep breath and sitting next to Leona on the rumpled bed. She launched into more questions.

"So what's your new roommate like?" Cassie asked. "Where did she come from? How did a first year get assigned to a third year, anyhow?"

Vega was staring at Cassie, willing her to slow down, but the girl was just getting started.

"You have to admit that it's a little weird that she doesn't have any belongings," Cassie added. "Where's her desk? Her bookcase? Her shelves?"

Leona stood up. "Did you come here to interrogate me about Ophelia?" she asked angrily. "Well, here's a star flash: I think she's great. She's sweet and the perfect roommate. Especially after that Scarlet," she spat out. "I'm so glad not to have to look at *her* weird stuff anymore."

"Leona, we were just—" Vega started.

"Ophelia's going to be back from the library soon, so why don't you just ask her yourself?" Leona interrupted. There was a grin on her face, but it looked angry and mocking. "Or better yet, why don't you just leave us both alone?"

"Sorry to have bothered you," Cassie muttered, jumping up from the bed. Vega followed her to the door, which Leona slid open with her wish energy manipulation skills. *She's good*, thought Vega. *Almost as good as I am.* Vega hurried into the hall, relieved to be out of the tense room. She felt lighter just standing in the hallway.

"Why are you bothering me, anyway?" Leona called after them. "You're just as annoying as Scarlet."

Cassie spun around so quickly that she knocked into Vega, who had to shoot out a hand and brace it against the wall to steady herself.

"Wait, you saw Scarlet?" they both cried.

But the door slid shut behind them with an angry bang.

CHAPTER 3

"**Well, that didn't go** very well," said Vega as the two girls, looking dejected, stood on the Cosmic Transporter on the way back to their dormitory.

After Leona kicked them out, they had stood there for a moment, wondering if they should knock and try to explain themselves. The door had slid open and they had smiled, eager to make amends. But Leona stuck her head out and said, "This isn't for you. Our scanner isn't working right and I have to leave it open for Ophelia in case I fall asleep before she gets back." She withdrew her head, then stuck it out again. "It's time for you to go."

Cassie had opened her mouth to reply, but Vega had stepped onto the Cosmic Transporter, pulling Cassie along with her. Enough was enough. Now Vega looked down at the smaller girl, who was frowning. "That must have been really hard for you," she told Cassie sympathetically. "You two were starting to become such good friends."

Cassie shrugged as if it didn't matter, but Vega was pretty sure she was still smarting. The girl's soft burgundy eyes flashed behind her large star-shaped glasses. "Well, at least now we know that Scarlet is still on campus!" she said. "I was afraid that she left the school."

Vega nodded. "We need to find her and see how she's doing." *And*, she added to herself, *convince her to rejoin the band.*

"Exactly!" said Cassie. "She needs to know that we're still her friends even if she isn't"—she lowered her voice—"officially one of us."

"I'll tell you one thing, though," Vega said thoughtfully, leaning on the railing. "Leona gets along really well with Ophelia, which is more than I can say for Piper and me these days, that's for sure." She turned to Cassie. "Hey, are you and Sage still bickering?"

Cassie opened her mouth to speak, then shut it.

"I said, are you and Sage still bickering?" Vega repeated.

Cassie's brow was furrowed. "I heard you the first time," she said. "And it just started me thinking. . . ." She looked down at her silver slippers, deep in thought, then lifted her head. "No," she said. "We've actually been getting along great. Ever since . . ."

"Ever since what?" Vega asked.

Cassie was nodding to herself. "That's so weird. I just realized the oddest thing. Sage and I have been getting along great ever since I got rid of that vase of flowers."

Vega made a face. "You mean those gorgeous coral flowers we all got? You got rid of them? Why would you do that? They're so pretty and they smell so good!"

Cassie tilted her head to the side. "They *were* pretty," she said. "And they did smell great." She paused for a moment to collect her thoughts. "And I can't really explain it, but I had this weird feeling about them. So one day I just threw them away. Sage was really mad at me at first and tried to get them back, but they had already vanished." Vega nodded. Once you put your refuse into a garbage can on Starland, it disappeared. Forever. "But she got over it amazingly quickly and we had a good laugh about it. And we've . . . we've gotten along ever since! How funny that I just put that together."

Vega barked out a laugh. "Oh, Cassie," she said. "Not to be rude or anything, but you have to admit that sometimes your hunches are totally wrong."

Cassie looked like she was about to argue, so Vega began to list examples. "Remember when you were convinced that the Bot-Bot waiter served you breakfast for dinner one night because it was mad at you, but it really just needed to be retuned?"

Cassie bit her lip. "Yeah," she said.

"Or when you thought that Lady Rancora stole your Star-Zap when it was obvious that she picked up the wrong one by accident?"

Cassie blushed. "Oh, you're right. I did act a little crazy then." Her determination returned. "But this time I'm pretty sure I'm on to something."

"I'm just saying that sometimes what seems like a hunch is just you being overly sensitive about things," Vega concluded. "And I just find it hard to believe that those gorgeous flowers we all got have some sort of power to make roommates argue with each other. Think about it. What would be the point? It's ridiculous!"

Cassie frowned. "I know it *sounds* strange," she said. "But I can't dismiss the fact that everything between us was better afterwards." She frowned. "But Leona and Ophelia are getting along great, right? I mean, she couldn't have stuck up for her any more than she did. And I know Leona had those flowers in her room. I saw them when they first got them. . . ." Her voice trailed off.

"That's true," said Vega. "So we're forgetting about that crazy idea?"

"Actually . . ." Cassie said with a frown, "I don't remember seeing any flowers in their room just now. Do you?"

Vega laughed. "I'm sure they had flowers, just like all of us." She thought for a moment. "In fact, I remember Scarlet complaining that they weren't black. Here, I'll prove it." She whipped out her Star-Zap and accessed the video album.

Cassie gave a low whistle. "Really, Vega? You holo-videoed the room? That's just weird."

Vega shrugged. "I holo-vid lots of things!" She turned it on and Cassie leaned over her shoulder to watch. She saw the strange room—half-messy, half-empty—come into view as the holo-camera scanned it and its contents (or lack thereof). Sure enough, the flowers were nowhere to be seen.

"See? No flowers," Cassie said triumphantly.

"I just can't believe that you think a vase of flowers could possibly make people not get along. It seems like a really big leap to take," said Vega.

Cassie stamped her foot. "I don't know why you can't see it! Sage and I and Leona and Ophelia are all getting along, and no one else is. It's so clear!"

Cassie certainly has a temper! thought Vega as they stepped off the Cosmic Transporter, pushed open the door to the dorm, and stepped outside. It was funny: the girl had been super shy at first, but when Cassie got to know someone, her true self certainly started to come out. They were greeted by the always soothing sound of the bloombugs' evening chorus. Cassie seemed to relax, for which Vega was grateful. Then came the sounds of students returning home for the evening; they chatted and laughed, their voices low and their bellies no doubt pleasantly full. The two girls paused for a moment between the dorm buildings, not quite ready to go inside the Little Dipper Dormitory. Vega squinted. "I think I see your roommate," she said. "Hey, what's that in the air following her?"

Cassie looked into the distance and grinned. "That's a Bot-Bot guide," she said. "MO-J4 to be precise. He has been following Sage everywhere, ever since she got back from her mission."

Vega guffawed. "I thought we weren't allowed to have pets on campus. That's grounds for automatic dismissal!"

Cassie' alabaster face grew even more pale, which seemed impossible to Vega. "It is?" she said worriedly.

"I was just joking," said Vega. "It is forbidden, of course, but the Student Handbook does not specifically mention automatic dismissal."

Cassie looked relieved.

Vega shook her head. "But Bot-Bots are like, neutral.

No emotions, you know? They certainly don't play favorites. They're supposed to help us all equally."

Cassie shrugged. "Well nobody told that to Mojo."

"Mojo?" said Vega. She gave Cassie a puzzled look.

"That's what he likes to be called," Cassie explained.

"*Likes* to be called?" Vega shook her head. This was highly irregular. "I don't get it," she said.

"Well, maybe it's because we're the Star Darlings," Cassie said with a shrug. "We're special."

But that didn't make sense to Vega. If MO-J4 was a special Star Darlings Bot-Bot, wouldn't he be following them all around? This was highly irregular and Vega didn't like it one bit. She shook her head as if to clear it and tipped it back to look at the stars which had just started to stud the darkening sky. Staring into the heavens always calmed her, and she brightened with an idea.

"Let's make a bet," she said to Cassie.

Cassie chuckled. "You and your games," she said, but her voice was kind. Perhaps the stars had settled her, as well.

"I just remembered that we have a botany lab on campus," said Vega.

"We do," agreed Cassie.

"So who better to tell us if there really is something odd about the flowers?" Vega asked.

Cassie nodded. "That's a great idea!"

Vega had a plan. "We can bring them in and leave them for observation," she suggested. "We won't say a word about them, just see what they can tell us. But here's the bet. If I'm right and they are simply ordinary flowers, you have to do a puzzle with me every starday for a double starweek."

Cassie sighed, but she was smiling. "Fine," she said. "But if *I'm* right and there's something wrong with the flowers, you have to help me with my Astral Accounting test. I'm just not absorbing the lessons the way I want to."

Vega would have helped Cassie with her Astral Accounting anyway (she adored numbers), but she simply said, "It's a deal." The two girls pressed their foreheads together, the traditional Starling way of sealing a deal.

Vega smiled. She knew that Cassie's imagination was getting away with her. The flowers would turn out to be normal, just as she thought, and she'd be able to share her rebuses and crossword puzzles with a friend for sixteen whole stardays. It was a win-win situation. They'd find Scarlet, and Leona would eventually return to her usual jovial self. Everything was going to be okay.

The two tore themselves away from the brilliant night sky and headed inside to the Cosmic Transporter, which would take them to their respective rooms.

"Good night," said Vega, who was dropped off first.

"Good night," said Cassie with a yawn. "I'll pick you— and the flowers—up in the morning before breakfast."

"See you tomorrow," said Vega. She placed her hand on the scanner and stepped inside. She checked the time on her Star-Zap. She'd be able to replay the day's lessons and listen to them twice before bed. Most students just listened to theirs at night as they slept. But Vega didn't like to take any chances. She wanted to graduate with top honors, and she'd do anything to make it happen. She put on her pajamas, sparkled her face, and brushed her teeth with her toothlight, then settled into bed with her earphones on. Piper, as usual, was already asleep.

★

Ding! Ding! Ding! Ding! Ding! Ding! Ding!

Cassie put her hand over the small bell that sat on the botany lab's front desk, to put an end to Vega's incessant ringing. The laboratory was located on the top floor of Halo Hall's science stellation, where the scientific departments and classrooms were located, and sunlight streamed through the glass roof, causing the two girls to squint at each other.

"That's enough, Vega!" Cassie said.

"Well, where are they?" Vega asked. She placed the

flowers on the desk. "We're going to miss breakfast. It's the most important meal of the day, you know." Although she was feeling quite impatient, she glanced around at the hydrongs of varieties of plants that filled the room. The botany lab boasted that it had a sample of every plant that grew on Starland, as well as several varieties that Starlings had brought back from trips to Wishworld, and it certainly appeared to be true. The air in the laboratory was moist and warm—pleasantly so, Vega thought—and the many blossoms perfumed the air with an intoxicating scent.

Vega spotted an interesting-looking specimen sitting on a shelf nearby. It was a short, squat, chubby plant and it looked tantalizingly fuzzy. *Go ahead, touch me*, it seemed to be saying. She reached out a finger toward the plant. . . .

"Careful!" someone said.

Vega jumped back and turned around. A woman in a white lab coat stood behind her, a blue holo–name tag pinned to her chest. Vega leaned forward and read it: GLADIOLUS ROSE, BOTANY LAB ASSISTANT.

"I'm Gladiolus Rose, botany lab assistant," she said unnecessarily. "Didn't mean to startle you," she added in an apologetic tone. "But I'd be careful if I were you. That's a cactus from Wishworld."

"What's a cactus?" asked Vega.

"Cactus plants are quite interesting, because they don't need much water. And they're very protective of themselves!" She laughed, waggling her bandaged fingers at Vega. "I learned the hard way. Those soft-looking hairs are really pointy little spikes that can get stuck in your skin!"

Vega backed away. "Thanks for the warning!" she said.

"Sorry for keeping you waiting," Gladiolus said. "I'm the only one on duty right now. Everyone else is attending a morning meeting, so I'm in charge of the lab at the moment. How can I help you?"

Vega lifted the vase of flowers off the desk. "We received these flowers as a gift. We don't recognize them and we were wondering if you could help us identify them," she said.

Gladiolus immediately looked intrigued. She reached for the vase and lifted it from Vega's hands. She studied the coral blossoms closely. "So interesting! They have the coloring of a roxylinda, but the flower is similar to a calliope," she said. She held up a single bloom. "But the leaves are more like those found on a violina. It's very intriguing! I don't think I've seen anything like this before. Perhaps it's some kind of new hybrid." She shook her head. "Of course," she added, "I'm still an assistant, so maybe one of the botanists will have a better idea of what these are. Can you leave them with us?"

"Yes," Vega and Cassie answered in unison.

Gladiolus leaned over and took a deep sniff. "I just can't stop smelling them. The scent is so similar to my favorite flower, the callistola, but they look nothing like them."

"Really?" said Cassie in disbelief. "I think they smell just like—"

Vega gave Cassie a gentle kick to stop her from talking. "I guess we'll be going now," she said. "We'll be in touch." She didn't want Cassie to give the assistant botanist any clues about the flowers.

Gladiolus smiled. "Startastic. This will be a fun challenge." She nodded, still staring at the flowers. "I'm . . . I'm almost compelled to keep sniffing them. It must be part of their makeup to attract insects to pollinate them. But how strange that it affects Starlings so strongly, as well! So interesting! Star salutations for bringing these in!"

The two girls said good-bye and left the lab. They broke into a jog when they realized how late it was, and raced each other to the Celestial Café. Most of their fellow Star Darlings had already finished their breakfast and set off for class. Only Clover remained, finishing a bowl of Sparkle-O's. The two girls placed a quick order with their hovering Bot-Bot waiter and soon received their astromuffins and glorange juice in to-go cups. They thanked the waiter.

"I wish you girls had time for a real meal," the Bot-Bot waiter said sadly, and they assured him they would make time for a proper breakfast the following morning. They munched their muffins on the way to class.

"So what class do you have now?" Vega asked before taking a long swig of juice.

"Wish Fulfillment," said Cassie with a smile. Professor Eugenia Bright was a captivating teacher and routinely won top honors as Starling Academy's favorite professor.

"Lucky," said Vega. "I have Wish Identification."

"With Professor Lucretia Delphinus?" asked Cassie. "Then you have my sympathies."

Tiny and tough, Professor Lucretia Delphinus was an inspiring teacher, but her temper could be mercurial. When she was in a happy mood, her class was a dream and Vega didn't want it to end. But if she was feeling cranky, everyone needed to watch out. On those days, Vega would sit through the whole class willing time to fly and trying hard not to steal glances at her Star-Zap to check on its progress. Once, Professor Lucretia Delphinus caught a student surreptitiously checking her Star-Zap, and she grabbed it from the girl and read the offending holo-text out loud. Most unfortunately, it had said DO YOU HAVE GOOD PLD OR BAD PLD FOR CLASS TODAY?

The girl had tried to explain that *PLD* stood for *Positive Light Definition*, but PLD herself would have none of it. There had been detention as a result—for everyone.

"I can't wait to find out what's going on with the flowers!" said Cassie excitedly, changing the subject. "The wait is going to kill me."

"Me too," said Vega teasingly. "I can't wait to discover that they're just ordinary flowers and that you'll be playing games with me all double starweek!"

Cassie shook her head. "Didn't you hear what she said? She'd never seen anything like them before!"

"Only because she's still an assistant," said Vega. "As soon as one of the real botanists takes a look, they'll identify them in no time."

Cassie shrugged. "I guess time will tell," she said. "How long do you think it will take? I wonder if we'll hear from them tomorrow. Do you th . . ." Her voice trailed off. "Vega? Vega, are you even listening to me?"

But Vega had just spotted a flash of pink and black ahead and wasn't listening at all. She grabbed Cassie's arm, dropping her half-eaten muffin. It fell to the floor unnoticed and was promptly squashed by a foot clad in a shiny bright-yellow shoe.

"Scarlet!" she managed to say. "I think I see Scarlet!"

Cassie's eyes lit up. "Where?" she asked eagerly.

"Up ahead!" Vega grabbed Cassie's hand, marveling briefly at how cold it was, and dragged her through the crowd, elbowing students out of her way in her excitement.

"Watch it!" said a fourth year with purple braids, turning around with a scowl.

"What's your hurry?" asked another as Vega accidentally knocked into her. "So rude!"

Cassie ducked under another girl's elbow as Vega spotted her target—a girl in a black miniskirt, pink-and-black-striped leggings, and a matching hoodie pulled over her head. Vega reached out and grabbed the girl's arm before she could disappear.

The girl spun around and smiled pleasantly at the two. "Hey, can I help you?" she asked, pulling down the hood and exposing her pale pink curls.

Vega felt the sinking feeling of disappointment in her stomach. "Starscuse me," she mumbled. "I thought you were someone else."

The girl nodded and turned away.

Cassie gave a strangled laugh. "She was much friendlier than Scarlet, anyway."

Vega grinned despite herself. "You're right."

The two girls stared at each other for a moment. Vega shrugged. "Oh, well," she said. "Here I am." She was standing right in front of her Wish Identification classroom. "See you last period," she told Cassie, and turned to go into the classroom.

"See you last period," said Cassie. Vega saw her own look of disappointment mirrored in the girl's expression.

"Vega! Starland to Vega!" someone said with exasperation.

Vega sat up straight with a start. She suddenly realized that every Starling in class was staring at her. The formidable professor was standing right in front of her, snapping her fingers in her face. *Oh, starf.*

"I'm sorry," she told the teacher, who was looking at her expectantly. "Can you repeat the question?"

Professor Lucretia Delphinus looked disappointed. "My most ardent student not paying attention," she said with a sigh. "And here I was, thinking that my lesson was particularly interesting today!"

Vega was deeply embarrassed and felt her cheeks flush hot and sparkly. She hated disappointing her teacher and being called out in front of the other students. She could imagine what they'd say: *See, she's one of those remedial class girls who don't belong. I knew she wasn't so smart after all!* But she had been mulling over the events of the past two days and had zoned out.

"I asked, 'Are you paying attention?'" Professor Lucretia Delphinus said with a smirk. "I guess I know what my answer is."

Half the class tittered, relieved that they weren't the ones caught in the starlight. The other half winced in sympathy.

"Sorry," said Vega.

"Not as sorry as I am," said Professor Lucretia Delphinus, which, as intended, made Vega feel even worse.

Vega was relieved to head to "remedial class" at the end of the day. She always felt much more relaxed when she was surrounded by her fellow Star Darlings. She settled herself in her chair, set her Star-Zap just so in the corner of her desk, and switched it on to begin recording so she wouldn't miss a word the teacher had to say when she arrived. Vega recorded everything, including the teacher's greeting and farewell, and appended her own thoughts to the recording. If a fellow student ever missed class, she always went to Vega, because Vega took the best and most thorough notes in the school.

The door slid open and the teacher stepped inside. Vega's heart sank. Was this a joke? That day's visiting lecturer was none other than Professor Lucretia Delphinus herself!

"Greetings, students," she said as she walked into the classroom briskly. The Star Darlings sat up straight and silenced themselves immediately. She smiled when she saw Vega giving her a sheepish look. "Vega! All has been forgiven," she said. "We start anew right now." Vega smiled back tentatively.

The professor sauntered down the aisle and paused at Vega's desk. "I'm only hard on you Star Darlings because I expect great things from you," she explained.

Vega nodded, relieved.

"Today we are going to concentrate on wish identification," she said. "This is the most difficult part of the wish-granting process." She looked around the room. "Why is that?" she asked.

Vega's hand shot up. She was eager to impress.

"Yes, Vega?"

"Because we don't receive a firm indication of when a wish is identified, the way we do when the Wisher is first identified. It can be different for everyone. Starlings have to rely on their gut feeling because they have no indication they are on the right track at all."

The professor nodded. Then someone caught her eye. "Ah, a new student," the teacher said. "What is your name?"

"Ophelia," the Starling answered, her cheeks flushed and sparkled.

"We'll start off with an easy question for you, Ophelia. How do you know when you have identified the correct Wisher?"

Ophelia looked panicked. "I . . . um . . . uh . . ." Shamefaced, she stared down at her desk. "I . . . uh . . . can't remember."

"Tsk, tsk, tsk," said the tiny teacher. "This is the difference between a successful mission and coming back from Wishworld with an empty Wish Pendant."

With a strangled sound, Leona stood up and ran out of the room.

Professor Lucretia Delphinus looked surprised. "Was it something I said?" she asked. She shrugged. "Vega, can you help Ophelia out?"

Vega could and did. She sat back in her seat, happy

to have redeemed herself. After class, she got an approving nod from the professor, and she left the room with a bounce in her step. Cassie caught up with her, her cheeks pink from exertion. After surreptitiously glancing around to make sure that Ophelia was not in earshot, she spoke.

"Excuse me?" asked Vega. She bent down closer to Cassie to hear better.

"Did you see that?" Cassie asked in a hushed voice. "It's so obvious that Ophelia shouldn't be here. I wish we could find Scarlet and tell her that!"

Vega shook her head. "Just because she's slow to catch on doesn't necessarily mean she's not Star Darlings material," she said. "But it would be great to find Scarlet and see if she knows why she was kicked out. I'm sure there's a perfectly rational explanation."

"If you say so," said Cassie. But to Vega, she did not look convinced one bit.

It was pretty clear that Cassie was not a morning person. Vega, on the other hand, was. She almost burst into laughter when she knocked softly on Cassie's door (so as not to disturb the still-sleeping Sage) bright and early the next morning and the girl emerged from her room.

Vega looked as crisp and neat as usual, wearing a blue tunic and footless tights, her usual serenely sophisticated style. Cassie, who tended to prefer dainty comfort in her outfits, walked out of the room with a scowl on her face, her pigtail buns askew, her dress tucked into her leggings, and two different silvery shoes on her feet. Vega untucked the girl's dress for her and pointed to her feet. Cassie glanced down, groaned, and returned to the room to find a matching pair of shoes.

But Cassie's grumpy expression began to relax as soon as they stepped outside into the early-morning starshine. They were headed to the botany lab to check on the flowers.

"Don't you think it's weird that we haven't heard from them yet?" Cassie asked as they boarded the Cosmic Transporter. Vega shortened her step a bit to match Cassie's stride.

"Maybe they're busy," suggested Vega. "Our flowers probably aren't too high on their priority list."

"Well, they should be," said Cassie grumpily. They exited the Cosmic Transporter in front of Halo Hall and walked up the white marble stairs.

When they reached the warm, moist lab, Cassie lunged forward and gave the bell a single polite ding before Vega could get her hands on it. A vase of crimsonalias sat on the desk nearby. Cassie gave Vega a look. *Don't even think about ringing that bell,* her expression seemed to say.

Gladiolus Rose strolled through a doorway, wiping her hands on her white lab coat. "Hello," she said. "How can I help you?"

Cassie gave Vega a glance. Didn't the assistant recognize them? It was almost as if she was meeting them for the first time.

"We, um, were just checking up on the flowers we dropped off the other day," Vega explained.

The woman looked behind her and lowered her voice. "I haven't shown them to anyone yet," she said. "The person I wanted to show them to, Professor Peony, has been in a terrible mood lately, so I didn't dare approach her."

"Gladiolus!" someone called out in a peevish tone.

Gladiolus rolled her eyes and began rearranging the bright red crimsonalias. "That's her," she said. "Looks like today isn't going to be any better." She leaned forward. "Listen, I'll try to show the flowers to her later today if I can. I promise!"

"Gladiolus!" Professor Peony called again, a rising note of annoyance in her voice.

"Coming!" Gladiolus called back loudly. She looked

down at her hands and realized she had snapped one of the crimsonalia branches in two. "My stars," she said. "Look, I've got to go. Why don't you come back in a couple of stardays, and I'll hopefully have an answer for you by then."

The two girls sighed. "Fine," said Cassie. As soon as Gladiolus left the room, Cassie whirled around to face Vega. "Did you hear that? They're arguing!"

Vega shook her head. "All I heard was one impatient professor. Hold your galliopes."

"Fine," said Cassie with a shrug. "We'll find out soon enough." She rubbed her hands together. "I can't wait till I'm proven right."

"Time will tell," said Vega. "You might just be joining me for sixteen straight stardays of puzzles."

"Oh, boy," said Cassie, feigning excitement.

"That's the spirit," said Vega with a grin.

They walked to the Celestial Café. The light wasn't flashing yet, so they settled themselves on the steps, which were cool, still holding a bit of the chill from the previous evening. Just then, Leona and Ophelia walked by, arm in arm. Cassie stiffened. Then she sighed. "I just miss my friend," she said. "And I'm worried about Scarlet. I wish things could go back to the way they used to be."

Vega laid a hand on Cassie's arm. "Everything is going to be okay," she said. She just hoped she was right.

The Star Darlings were quieter than usual that morning at breakfast. They all seemed to have a lot on their minds. But the air of melancholy didn't do anything to affect Vega's appetite. She quickly polished off her order of starcakes and was wiping her chin with her napkin, about to starscuse herself from the table, when there was a muted buzzing noise, like a swarm of happy glitterbees discovering a bluebeezel garden.

Twenty-four eyes widened and twelve hands reached out to grab their Star-Zaps in unison.

S.D. WISH ORB IDENTIFIED. PROCEED TO LADY STELLA'S OFFICE IMMEDIATELY.

From the other side of the table, there was an excited yelp, which was quickly hushed. Adrenaline coursed through Vega's veins, and it took all her will to keep herself from jumping out of her seat and running as fast as her legs would carry her to Lady Stella's office. That wasn't allowed. She breathed in and out deeply several times to maintain her focus. The other Star Darlings were also admirably composed. Either alone or in pairs, the girls pushed out their chairs, stood, and strolled out of the cafeteria casually—chatting to one other, grabbing an extra astromuffin, looking like it was just another day. Vega glanced around at everyone, fully aware that behind their calm exteriors, they were all just as tense and excited as she was. *We should join the acting club when this is all over,* thought Vega. *We're naturals!*

Vega arrived in Lady Stella's office right after Leona and Ophelia and just before Clover. They filed in and took their usual seats. As Vega drummed her fingers impatiently on the table, Libby twirled a piece of her pink hair around her finger, Leona scowled, Ophelia looked positively terrified, and Adora hummed tunelessly. "Stop it," snapped Tessa, and the two started to argue.

Then Lady Stella appeared in the doorway and everyone immediately hushed. Tall and regally beautiful, she wore a silver turban, and her lips were painted a brilliant shade of red. She spread her arms, her full sleeves ballooning out at her sides. She looked down at them with a tender smile.

"I realize you're all very excited and tense," she said. "But Star Darlings must always be respectful of each other. I just want to remind you that you were chosen not for your singularities but because of the way the twelve of you fit together, like the pieces of a puzzle. You must support each other at all times, not tear each other down."

Vega looked around the table. Everyone was rapt. She marveled at how even when they were being scolded by Lady Stella, everyone still looked grateful to have her attention.

"We're sorry, Lady Stella," said Tessa. Everyone murmured agreement.

Lady Stella clasped her hands. "As you know, a Star Darlings' Wish-Watcher has spotted a Wish Orb that has begun to glow," she told them. "This means that a Wisher's wish is ready to be granted, and one of you is the perfect Starling to fulfill that wish. One of you"— she paused—"will shortly be on your way to Wishworld to begin a journey that, if all goes well, will be beneficial to both you and your Wisher. And Starland itself, of course," she added. "Now we will head to the Star Caves once more for the Wish Orb presentation."

Lady Stella realized that one student was looking quite confused. She smiled at her kindly. "This is all new to you, Ophelia," she said to the new Star Darling. "You see, underneath the school are secret caves known only to me, the Star Darlings, and a special few of my trusted advisors. That is where we have our own secret Wish-House, where special Wish Orbs are planted. When a Wish Orb begins to glow, we hold a secret ceremony to determine which of you is best suited for the mission based on your talents and the nature of the wish."

Ophelia nodded mutely, her face drawn. She made Cassie, who (as usual) looked slightly ill at the possibility of going down to Wishworld, look starmendously excited in comparison.

Lady Stella walked to her desk, pulled open the top drawer, and reached inside. A hidden door in the back wall slid open and Ophelia gasped. A faint musty chill snuck into the room. Silently, the Star Darlings stood and made their way to the door in a calm and orderly fashion. There was no pushing or shoving or arguing as each girl patiently waited her turn to pass through the doorway and carefully made her way down the circular staircase, gripping the cold banister. Vega heard someone say, "After you, of course," and someone else said, "No, you first," and she grinned, knowing that the girls were going out of their way to show Lady Stella just how civilized and supportive they could be. The hard soles of Vega's blue clogs made sharp ringing sounds on the metal stairs. She felt light-headed, and the hand not clutching the banister was all fluttery, like it was trying to escape from the end of her arm. *I've never felt quite this nervous before*, she thought, surprised by her reaction. *Just* before every other Wish Orb presentation, she had been as matter-of-fact as usual. She wasn't sure what was going on with her this time.

At the bottom of the steps, she jumped when Cassie put a cold hand around hers and gave it a squeeze. She smiled at her friend's thoughtfulness, especially since she knew how nervous Cassie must be.

"I'm sorry Scarlet isn't here," said Cassie in a low voice. "She loves these caves."

Leona turned around and scowled at them both. Vega ignored her and looked around the gloomy space, not certain what Scarlet found so appealing about the caves. They were dank and drippy, and they smelled old and musty. Strange creatures inhabited the dark corners, and you never knew when one might dart out and run across your foot, its claws scrabbling over your instep. She shivered at the thought, then had a sudden realization: that was exactly why the dark and mysterious Scarlet liked the caves, actually!

They walked through the gloom single file as Lady Stella led them down several twisty hallways, then came to a stop in front of a nondescript door. Vega blinked. She was fairly certain they had come an entirely different way the time before. The headmistress pushed open the door and grinned as glorious sunshine poured into the dark hallway. Ophelia gasped. And just like that, the flutterfocuses that had been dancing around in Vega's stomach vanished. That was exactly what was supposed to happen; she could feel it. She was suddenly, strangely, gloriously calm. She had this. She just knew it.

CHAPTER
4

And as she would soon find out, she was right. She watched as Ophelia gaped at the room. They were standing in a special Wish-House that had been built just for them. Although they were deep underneath Halo Hall, they could still look up through the glass roof and see blue sky and puffy white clouds drifting by.

"But . . . but . . . but it's impossible!" Ophelia said.

Leona shrugged. "Impossible . . . yet here we are," she replied.

Lady Stella led them to the center of the room, and they all grouped around the raised platform, where the Wish Orb would appear.

Lady Stella cleared her throat and Vega turned her attention to the headmistress. "As you know, or don't yet," she said, indicating Ophelia, "the Wish Orb will choose which of you is the best match for its wish." She clapped her hands and the room darkened. A beam of light shot down from above and illuminated the middle of the platform. It opened and a single Wish Orb appeared. There was a sharp intake of breath. Although they all (except Ophelia, of course) had seen this three times now, it was still a magical sight. The Wish Orb was round and looked like a beautiful iridescent bubble made of the finest spun glass. It glowed with remarkable intensity. There was a slight breeze, warm and refreshing at the same time, and the orb began to move around the platform, pausing for a moment in front of each girl. Adora held out her hand as if to touch it, and the look of sadness on her face when it moved away was heartbreaking. Leona looked away as it passed, as if it pained her too much to see the orb. Cassie let out a large sigh as it went by (of relief, Vega was sure of it). The orb paused in front of Vega, and she held her breath, steeling herself for the disappointment she would feel if it moved on to the next Star Darling. But that moment never came. Vega looked at Lady Stella questioningly. The headmistress beamed, leaned over, and took the orb carefully in her hands. It lit up her beautiful face, and she turned to Vega. Her eyes sparkled with pleasure as she said, "The orb has chosen. It's yours, Vega."

Vega set three separate alarms on her Star-Zap that night, but she didn't need any of them, for Piper woke her up at the crack of dawn, talking in her sleep. Or to be more specific, yelling.

It was mostly gibberish and made no sense to Vega, but a couple of the words were clear: *help, stop,* and was that *thief*? Rubbing sleep from her eyes, Vega swung her legs out of bed, crossed the room, and shook Piper's shoulder, perhaps a bit more roughly than she intended. "Wake up!" Vega said. "You're dreaming!"

The sparkle of the morning stars was just starting to peek over the horizon, and the room was still deep in shadows. Vega switched on a light. She saw that Piper's eyes were open, but she was staring at Vega confusedly, like she didn't recognize her. Her cheeks were flushed and she had a terrified look on her face, her eyes darting around the room. "She stole my Wish Pendant! Where is my Wish Pendant?" she cried, looking around wildly. Vega still wasn't sure Piper knew where she was or even who Vega was. It was a little scary.

Vega's arm shot out and she began frantically rummaging around on Piper's nightstand, knocking over a glass of water. (It instantly dried, as spills always did on Starland.) Where was her Wish Pendant? Finally, her fingers closed on the cool metal of the bracelet. She held it aloft. "Here it is," she said soothingly. "Piper, it was only a dream." She slipped it onto Piper's wrist, which seemed to calm her immediately.

An expression of great relief flooded Piper's face. But then she looked up at Vega reproachfully. "Only a dream? Really? You know how important dreams are!" she said coldly. "Especially to me!"

Vega shrugged. "Sorry," she said. "I . . . I wasn't thinking."

Piper sat up in bed, her fingers tightly wrapped around her Wish Pendant, as if the dream villain was going to reappear and try to wrest it away from her.

"Hand me my dream diary!" Piper demanded. This was very unlike her, and Vega stared for a moment. Piper corrected herself immediately. "Um, would you mind getting me my dream diary?" she asked sheepishly.

"Sure," said Vega. She hurried across the room and grabbed the top holo-diary in the basket. She handed it to Piper, who grasped it in her hands and closed her eyes, clearly trying hard to recall the dream. She finally tossed down the diary in frustration. "I can't remember!" she said sadly. "It's slipping away. All I can recall is that someone was chasing me, trying to take my Wish Pendant. I stopped to rest and they grabbed it." She thought hard. "I can't remember the face. Or even if it was a man or a woman. But it seemed so real. . . ." Her voice trailed off.

Vega shivered. Piper was usually all relaxation and sleeping masks but at times could get quite creepy without warning. This was one of those times.

Vega looked at Piper for a moment, trying to return her to reality. "Well, I guess it's time to get ready for my Wish Mission," she said. No reaction. "My Wish Mission to Wishworld," she said loudly. Piper still sat up in bed, staring into space. *All this drama over a silly dream!* Vega thought. *She* was the one who should be anxious this morning, not Piper!

But it didn't register with Piper. She slowly stood up and walked to the sparkle shower room. "I'll take a sparkle shower now," she said. "Maybe that will help calm me down."

Vega shook her head. She had assumed it would go without saying that she would get to take the first sparkle shower of the day. She laughed. It wasn't like she had big plans or anything. She was just going to hitch herself to a blazing shooting star and hurtle down to a distant world. No big deal.

While she waited her turn, she neatened the already spotless room, returning Piper's holo-diary to the basket and making both of their beds. Piper's soft seafoam green sheets were so tangled up Vega wondered if she had actually been running in her sleep. She accessed the Wishworld Outfit Selector but, after flipping through various options, decided she was happy with the choice she had made the previous night.

Vega stood over her bedside table, staring down at her Star-Zap. Her mother's face surrounded by a red star still sat in the corner of the screen, indicating the unreturned holo-call. She briefly considered calling her back, as it would be comforting to see her mom's face before her mission, despite the questions she would have to answer about scheduling a visit and the half-truths she would have to tell about her schooling. But then the sparkle shower room door slid open and Piper stepped out, a fresh glow on her skin.

"I feel much better," she told Vega.

"Great," Vega replied.

Vega abandoned her phone, grabbed her soft blue bathrobe, and stepped into the sparkle shower room. She glanced at the mirror. Her shiny blue hair was slightly mussed, and she smoothed it. Her bright blue eyes, the color of cloud-free skies, stared back at her. She was surprised to realize she still felt calm and relaxed. She took a long sparkle shower, even though she knew she would shortly be transforming her skin from sparkly to dull. It still was invigorating and good for the spirits. She slipped on a loose blue dress with a turquoise starburst on the front and a pair of pretty sandals. When Piper was ready, the two girls headed to the Celestial Café. The Star Darlings had all been instructed the day before to have a quick but nutritious breakfast and head straight to the private balcony of the Wishworld Surveillance Deck to see Vega off before classes began. As Vega approached the table, she was surprised to notice that the other Star Darlings looked more nervous than she felt. Leona appeared particularly out of sorts, staring down at her glass of glorange juice and not engaging in conversation with anyone—not even Ophelia, who looked more lost and lonely than usual. Maybe Leona was jealous of Vega's mission? Resentful that Vega was likely to collect wish energy? Or just feeling sad that her mission had not gone well and she most likely would not get a chance at redemption? Vega wasn't sure and she certainly wasn't going to ask.

There was a tray of baked goods in the middle of the table, and Vega grabbed a fruit bun and sank her teeth into it, then licked her hand as a blob of ozziefruit jam leaked out. *Yum.* Glancing down at her Star-Zap, Vega realized it was already time to go to the deck. She stood, her chair making a loud scraping sound on the floor. Cassie nodded at her across the table. Vega left the room, knowing that the other eleven would soon be following her, drifting out casually in groups of two and three so as not to arouse any suspicion from their fellow students.

She walked a little more quickly than usual and hopped into an empty Flash Vertical Mover car and pressed the button. The doors slid shut and she took a deep breath, enjoying the solitude. The Wishworld Surveillance Deck towered ridiculously high above the campus, but the Flash Vertical Mover zoomed her up in mere starsecs. She swallowed hard to keep her ears from popping. Soon she was stepping out onto the deck. She had it all to herself, and she stood there for a moment, marveling at the view. It never ceased to amaze her that far below on Wishworld, Wishlings were living their lives, going to school, and making the wishes that kept life on Starland proceeding as usual. And soon she would be a crucial part of one Wishling's life, if only for a short time. She took a deep breath and monitored how she felt again. Fine—no flutterfocuses in the stomach, trembling hands, or racing thoughts. She was ready and confident in her ability to take on any challenge she was given.

The door opened and Tessa and Gemma joined her on the private balcony. Gemma opened her mouth to begin her usual chattering, but her older sister shushed her. Vega gave Tessa a grateful glance. She was quickly realizing that the time just before you took off on a Wish Mission was sacred and special, meant to be savored.

Lady Stella appeared, almost out of thin air. "Hello, Vega," she said. Her eyes were kind and warm. She squeezed Vega's shoulder and leaned down to speak to her privately. "You have the skills, you have the brains, and you certainly have the drive, my dear," she said. "Just make sure to see the forest for the trees. Don't get too caught up in the details, and try to see the bigger picture. This mission is tailor-made for you."

Vega felt warm pride rush through her. "Thank you for your confidence," she said.

The door opened and the rest of the Star Darlings spilled onto the balcony and clustered around Vega, giving her effusive hugs and showering her with good wishes. It was a little disorganized, and just as Vega began to feel overwhelmed by all the attention, Cassie noticed and stepped in, lining everyone up to say their farewells in an orderly fashion. Vega smiled at her friend in thanks.

Piper approached Vega, a slightly sleepy look still in her eyes. She grasped both of Vega's hands in her own. "I was so worked up this morning I totally forgot about your mission," she said, looking ashamed. "Good luck, Vega."

Adora gave her a quick firm squeeze. "You'll be a superstar," she said. "There's no doubt about that."

Leona was next. "I hope you are able to collect wish energy," she said sadly. "Keep your eye on your Wish Pendant."

"I will," Vega promised her.

Libby said, "Take it from me: make sure to double-check that you have the right wish!"

"And the right Wisher," added Sage, poking her head over Libby's pink shoulder.

"Star salutations to you both," Vega said. She was touched that the girls were so willing to point out their mistakes to help her.

Gemma and Tessa stepped up to Vega together. "You're going to be startastic," Gemma told her. "Out of this world. The Wisher who gets you as their

Wish-Granter is going to be absolutely starstruck! As a matter of fact—"

Tessa interrupted. "As a matter of fact, good luck from both of us," she said, dragging her sister away. She called back, "Don't forget to bring back some of that chocolate Sage talked so much about if you can!"

Cassie simply gave Vega a kiss on the cheek.

Ophelia was the last to approach Vega. "You don't look scared at all," she said shyly. Her large ochre eyes were wide with wonder. "Now how do you get down to Wishworld again?"

Before Vega could answer, Lady Cordial appeared and handed Vega her backpack. It was a pretty blue with a glittery star on it.

"Star salutations," said Vega.

Lady Cordial, who was perhaps nervous she would start stuttering, as she often did when she was around large groups of Starlings, simply nodded.

"Vega! We need you!" Lady Stella called from the edge of the roof. "The Star Wranglers have spotted a shooting star!" The crowd parted as Lady Stella held out her hand. It was almost as if things were happening in slow motion for Vega. She stepped forward to join Lady Stella and watched in silence as the wranglers tossed out the lasso and just missed catching the star. It hurtled through the heavens and disappeared. "Awww!" everyone said. Luckily, the wranglers spotted another one almost immediately. They tossed out their lasso again and caught it. Sparks shot out as it strained against its restraints. Burning bright and beautiful, the star hovered in the air before them as the wranglers struggled to keep it steady.

Once Vega was safely attached, she paused to take one last look at everyone, their faces hopeful and concerned. "Good-bye!" she called. "I'll do everyone pr—" Then her words were lost in a loud *whoosh* as she was released into the heavens, the wranglers no longer able to keep their grip on the star, which was desperate to continue its fiery arc.

Vega zoomed through the sky as whirling multicolored lights, intense fiery flares, and twinkling stars flashed by. But despite the distractions, she was somehow able to remain studiously focused on her Star-Zap. (She had made this journey once before, when she had helped Leona.) As soon as the screen began to flash COMMENCE APPEARANCE CHANGE, she was ready. She concentrated hard and could see from an errant wisp near the corner of her eye that her hair had changed from cerulean to a very dark brown—almost black. She pressed a button on her Star-Zap and was instantly wearing the outfit she had carefully picked out the night before—a skirt made out of a rough material the Wishlings called denim, a simple blue-and-white-striped long-sleeved T-shirt, and a matching denim vest. On her feet she wore pretty blue woven shoes called espadrilles. She put her hand on her Wish Pendant, which was the sparkling buckle of her belt, and began to say the words that would begin the last step of her physical transformation: "Star light, star bright, first star I see tonight: I wish I may, I wish I might, have the wish I wish tonight." The Wish Pendant began to glow, and she gasped as the glitter was swept off her skin in a sudden rush of warm air.

PREPARE FOR LANDING, the Star-Zap read. Before she knew it, the surface of Wishworld was rushing up to meet her. She held her breath and landed gently in a grassy park. She blinked for a moment, taking in her surroundings, and let out her breath in one big whoosh. She hadn't realized she was still holding it. It appeared that she had landed in a park at the bottom of a large landmass surrounded by water. The park was empty save a mother sitting on a bench next to a baby stroller, her back to Vega. The child, who had apparently witnessed Vega's arrival, pointed at her and said, "Star."

"That's right," said the mother in a loud sunny voice,

pointing to a nearby yellow vehicle driving by on the street. "Car!"

Following the instructions she had been given, Vega waited until the star had sputtered out, then picked it up and began to fold it. When it was the size of a wallet and could not fold any more, she placed it in the front zippered portion of her backpack. She looked at her Star-Zap for further instructions. PROCEED DIRECTLY TO THE GEORGE ROBERT INTERNATIONAL SCHOOL FOR GIRLS, it said. Detailed directions followed, along with an estimated walking time of thirty starmins. Vega looked at her pretty shoes and immediately accessed her Wishworld Outfit Selector. She switched to a pair of blue sneakers and was off!

The farther uptown Vega walked, the bigger the buildings became and the more crowded the streets got. She stared openly at people and no one seemed to care or notice. She passed stores, gaping doorways that led to deep stairwells labeled SUBWAY, small parks filled with what looked like the youngest and oldest Wish-lings and their respective caretakers, and lots of vehicles of all shapes and sizes, none self-driving. This part of Wishworld was noisier, dirtier, and stinkier than the first Wishworld place she had visited during Leona's mission. It was also much busier and more vibrant, she had to give it that.

Finally, she arrived at the school. The large, impressive white stone building stood in the middle of the city block. She admired the tall steps, the supporting columns. It reminded her a bit of Halo Hall. The street in front of the school was packed with idling cars, waiting to pick up students, she assumed.

She stole a glance at her Star-Zap and noted the time: 3:01 P.M. Just then, the doors burst open and students began to trickle out. Within moments the trickle became a flood.

Vega, who had just begun to climb the stairs, was pushing against the tide. A girl, her eyes glued to her phone, came straight toward her, and Vega stepped neatly out of the way, bumping right into someone else. "Starscu . . . I mean, excuse me," Vega said, but the girl didn't seem to hear. Forcing her way through the onslaught of students, she squeezed inside the door and found herself in the crowded school vestibule. She blinked, trying to get her bearings. A sign on the wall caught her eye. AFTER-SCHOOL CLUBS, it said, with an arrow pointing up. She looked down at her Wish Pendant, which was beginning to glow very faintly.

After-school clubs, here I come, she thought, taking the stairs marked *up*, which were empty, two at a time. (The stairs marked *down* were bustling with students.) She reached the second floor and pushed open the heavy door. There she found a woman in a navy jacket sitting behind a table, a clipboard in front of her. She was speaking to a boy holding a potted plant. "The Venus Flytrap Club is in room 222," she told him. She turned to Vega. "Welcome!" she said, looking over her glasses at her. "How can I help you?"

"I am Vega. I am a new student."

The woman nodded. "You are Vega. You are a new student," she said automatically.

"Which club are you headed to?" the woman asked. That question stumped Vega. What kinds of clubs did Wishlings have? Was there a star-ball club? A wish energy manipulation club? Probably not.

"Oh," Vega said, smiling. She made a guess. "Puzzle Club?"

The woman's brow furrowed and she scanned her list. She looked up. "No, no Puzzle Club. Though that does sound like fun," she said. "Are you sure that's the right club?"

Vega thought again. "Ahhh, ahhhh . . ."

"Acrobatics Club?" the woman suggested helpfully.

It was as good as any. "That's it!" said Vega.

"Room 212," the woman said. "Right down the hallway." As Vega turned away, she heard the woman say, "Mmmmm, I smell pound cake!" *So it's true*, Vega thought. To Wishling adults, Starlings smelled like their favorite baked good from childhood. *Maybe to put them at ease or something*, Vega thought. It was odd but kind of nice when you thought about it. Her very presence brought back pleasant childhood memories.

Vega glanced down at her belt buckle Wish Pendant and noticed that the glow was a bit brighter than before. She paused in front of room 212. What were the chances that her Wisher would be in this club? She shrugged and opened the door. At least it was a start.

The floor of room 212 was covered with thick padded mats. Girls wearing tightly fitting shirt-underwear combinations were sitting on the mats, doing splits and stretching. Vega found their costumes to be very odd and was a little taken aback that no one was wearing pants.

A girl in a red, white, and blue underwear suit turned to her. "Hey," she said. "You must be new. Welcome!" She looked Vega up and down. "Where's your leotard?"

"My what?" asked Vega. *Mission 4, Wishworld*

Observation #1: Some Wishlings wear a legless article of clothing called a leotard. Function: unclear at this point.

The girl laughed, apparently assuming Vega was kidding with her. "No worries," she said.

"Oh, I wasn't worried," Vega assured her.

The girl laughed again. "We usually start with some headstands," she informed Vega. "Then we move on to forward rolls, bridges, handstands, back flips, and then we end with a pyramid!"

Vega raised her eyebrows. "Oh," she said. It sounded very busy. She watched as the girl dropped to the ground, placed her head on the floor, and balanced her knees on her elbows before extending her legs straight up into the air. Once she was certain of her balance, she began bending her legs in different poses. The other girls followed suit.

Vega was game. After several attempts, she was able to shakily stand on her head. She felt very proud of herself in the split second before she spilled onto the floor. She put her head back down and was face-to-face with her middle, about to balance her knees on her elbows, when she realized that her belt, mere inches from her face, was no longer glowing. *It's been fun, Acrobatics Club,* she thought as she got to her feet. *But I have to move on.*

With an apologetic grin, she headed toward the door. The girl who had first welcomed her looked at Vega as if she had betrayed her. "We were going to put you on top of the human pyramid!" she said.

"Maybe next time," said Vega. She shuddered at the thought, relieved to be dodging that experience.

Once she was back in the hallway, her Wish Pendant began to glow faintly again. Her Wisher was near. There was no question about it. She just needed to be patient.

Vega decided to try the classroom next door. She opened the door, and the teacher and two students looked up eagerly from the bucket they were inspecting. Vega stared. What could possibly be going on there?

"Welcome to Composting Club!" the teacher said.

"Is everyone here?" Vega asked.

"Um, yes," the teacher said. She laughed sheepishly. "We're a small club."

Vega looked down at her pendant. No glow at all.

"Sorry!" she said, starting to close the door. The students looked disappointed for a moment but immediately returned to examining the bucket. Vega never found out exactly what was inside. *Mission 4, Wishworld Observation #2: Composting Club does not seem very popular. Look into this.*

She watched with interest as several students parried in the Fencing Club, their faces obscured by strange masks. Her eyes widened as students pantomimed being trapped in invisible boxes, pulled ropes she couldn't see, and walked into a nonexistent gust of wind in Mime Club. And the smells coming from Cooking Club were tantalizing. But she was on a mission. Until the light glowed on her pendant, she had to keep looking. *Just how many clubs does this school have, anyway?* she wondered.

"Forty-seven," someone said.

Vega spun around. She hadn't realized she had said the words out loud. A girl stood in front of her, her orangey hair cascading down her back in rippling curls. Her eyes were bright blue and her pretty face was covered in freckles that reminded Vega of constellations.

"How many clubs did you say?" Vega asked.

"Forty-seven," the girl repeated.

"That's a lot of clubs," Vega said shakily.

The girl grinned. "There's something for everyone," she said. "And then some." She cocked her head at Vega. "So let me guess. You're new and haven't found the right club yet?"

"That's right. I'm Vega, by the way."

The girl stuck out her hand. "Katie."

Vega recalled immediately that she was supposed to

grasp and pump the hand, otherwise known as "shaking." Libby had certainly made a mess of that on her Wish Mission! While Vega made contact, she took a quick glance at her Wish Pendant, which told her that this girl was not her Wisher. Too bad. She seemed nice.

Katie smiled at Vega. "You want to join a really fun club? Come with me," she said. She set off down the hallway. Not knowing what else to do, Vega followed her.

CHAPTER
5

Katie pushed open the door to room 261. "Come right in," she said. About ten students sat in a circle. Vega stared at them. They had large balls of thick string in their laps and long sticks in their hands. They moved the sticks back and forth. It was very strange.

"What club is this?" Vega asked.

Katie laughed. "You're so funny! What else could it be? It's Knitting Club, of course!"

Vega knew that the only reason she was making everyone laugh was that she didn't understand Wishling ways, but she still enjoyed it, basking in the warm glow of her classmates' grins. Back home she was the serious one; on Wishworld she already had a reputation as a joker. It felt good to be thought of as funny.

"Welcome," said the teacher, a tall thin woman with curly brown hair and thick glasses. "I assume you know how to cast on?" She handed Vega her own ball of string and two of the pointy sticks. "You can borrow these for today. Next week you should bring your own yarn and needles."

Vega knew that no matter what happened, good or bad, the Countdown Clock would have run out of time before next week's class. Still, she nodded in agreement. She was afraid to ask what "casting on" was, in case it was a special Wishling skill that everyone was born with. So she stared at the needles and the ball of yarn, willing herself to figure out how to do it. As you might imagine, that didn't work. Not about to waste any of her precious wish energy in the attempt to acquire knowledge, she decided she'd fake it. But she had no idea what to do. She was tempted to leave the room and consult her Star-Zap for possible directions, but then she glanced down at her lap and saw her Wish Pendant. It was glowing! Her Wisher was near. Startastic!

She looked around the room eagerly. Who could it be? The girl with the long dark hair and nervous laugh who was knitting so quickly her needles flashed? The girl with the short blond hair who was creating what looked like the world's longest (and lumpiest) scarf? Or maybe it was the girl who was sitting next to her, scowling as she ripped out a row of stitches?

Keep cool, Vega, she said to herself. *You'll figure it out.* She remembered what she had learned in Wishers 101 class: FIGGO—Fitting In Guarantees Good Outcome. She picked up the needles and began to wrap the yarn around them. *Maybe this is how you start,* she thought in desperation.

She looked at Katie for help. But she was talking a mile a minute to another girl and gesturing with one of her needles. The other girl was half-listening, a nervous eye trained on the moving needle in Katie's hand.

Vega stared down at her own needles helplessly.

"Hey, do you need help?" someone asked.

She looked up hopefully. A girl was smiling down, peering at her from behind funny-shaped eyeglasses without any lenses in them, her curly black hair cut with uneven bangs and one side longer than the other. Always-precise Vega was surprised to find that rather than looking strange, the haircut gave the girl an endearingly off-kilter look. Her simple black sweater had a bright pink fuzzy neckline. She wore a slim black skirt and bright pink tights, and her chunky black boots looked artfully beat-up. They were embellished with bright paint splatters. Vega looked at her admiringly.

Vega was more of a dress-for-comfort kind of girl, but even she could tell the girl had style.

"I just finished my project, a shrug," she said, holding up an adorable abbreviated sweater that had only arms and shoulders. It was made out of glittery maroon wool. "I don't have anything to do, so I'm all yours!" She sat down in the chair next to Vega's. "Give me your hand," she said. Vega obeyed, and the girl laid the end of the yarn on Vega's palm, looped over itself. "Now watch," she said, sticking her fingers through the loop and pulling the yarn through. "See? A slipknot. That's how you start."

She took Vega's knitting needle and poked it through the hole. Then she showed her how to cast on, making an X with the needles, looping the yarn around the back needle, pulling it underneath, and then slipping the other needle through to steal it back.

"Now you try," she said.

Vega stuck out her tongue in concentration. After a couple of false starts, she began to get the hang of it. She smiled. It was an odd Wishling pastime, but she could see its appeal. *Mission 4, Wishworld Observation #3: Knitting seems complicated, but it's not as hard as it looks. It's actually quite relaxing!*

"Hey, you're a good teacher," she said. "What's your name? I'm Vega."

"Hello, Vega," the girl said. "I'm Ella. So, are you ready to knit?"

Vega nodded. It was the same process, except after you pulled the stitch underneath, you slipped it off one of the needles and onto the other.

"I'm knitting!" Vega cried.

"Amazing," said the girl. "You're a quick learner. Once you do a couple of rows, I'll teach you how to purl." She looked down at Vega's waist. "Hey," she said. "What a cool belt buckle! How does it glow? Does it have a battery or is it solar powered?"

Vega nearly dropped her knitting as she looked down at her belt. It was definitely glowing. Still, better safe than sorry. Her eyes on the belt, she walked away from Ella and stood next to another girl, who looked up at her in confusion. The belt buckle dimmed. She sidled up to Ella, who had started knitting again. It glowed once more. Ella smiled and shook her head. "You're so funny!" she said.

There it was again! Vega grinned. She was having the best time on Wishworld. She had learned to knit, found her Wisher, and made several Wishlings laugh.

Her mission was off to a startastic start!

When Knitting Club was over, Vega returned the needles and yarn to the teacher and promised (falsely) that she would bring her own supplies the next week. Then she turned around to look for Ella. But Ella was gone.

Vega ran to the top of the stairs. She spotted Ella's pink collar and multicolored boots just as they disappeared through the door.

"Ella! Wait!" she called. Vega ran down the steps, but when she pushed open the door, her Wisher was nowhere to be found. There was a line of cars waiting to pick up students. *Ella must be in one of them*, she thought. She stepped off the curb and tried peering through the windows of one. But all she could see was her own curious face and dark brown hair, which she still hadn't gotten used to. It was impossible to see inside the car.

The window rolled down. It was Katie. "Hey, Vega, are you looking for your driver?" the girl asked.

"Um . . . no," said Vega. "Just looking for Ella."

"Don't know what to tell you. She disappeared," said Katie with a shrug. "She's good at that."

"Okay, thanks," said Vega. She turned to walk away.

"Hey, do you need a ride somewhere?" Katie asked, leaning her head out the window.

Vega looked down the street one last time. But Ella was definitely gone. "Um, sure. As long as your dad doesn't mind," she said, indicating the man who sat behind the wheel.

Katie laughed. "You crack me up. You know that's my driver!"

Katie opened the door and slid over. As Vega settled into the soft black seat, Katie handed her a black buckle on a strap.

"Thanks," said Vega, taking it from her and holding on to it.

Katie looked at her funny.

"What?" said Vega.

Katie burst into laughter. "Oh, Vega!" she said fondly. She reached across her and snapped it into the latch. The strap felt snug against Vega's torso.

"Oh, it's a restraining device!" she said. Self-driving Starland cars never, ever got into accidents, so Starlings were free to move about in their vehicles at all times. Vega felt oddly constrained but didn't say anything.

Katie smiled. "So how did you like Knitting Club?" she asked. "I was right, pretty fun, huh?"

"Yeah," said Vega. "I liked it." Then she added, "So, um, what's Ella like?"

"Oh, she's really nice. She's in my class," Katie said.

Vega sat up straight. "Oh, really?" she said. "Uh . . . me too!"

"You are?" said Katie. She shrugged. "That's cool. She's new this year. She has all these great outfits, because her mom is a famous fashion designer." She looked embarrassed. "I actually tried to Google her mom once, but I couldn't find anything. She must be, like, totally exclusive."

Google? Vega tried to look wise. She nodded. "Totally. Well, that makes sense, about her mom being a fashion designer, that is. She did have on a startas—I mean, a fantastic outfit."

"It was pretty sick," said Katie.

Vega stared at her. Perhaps Katie had misunderstood her. "Oh, no, I meant that I enjoyed it," Vega explained.

Katie grinned and gave Vega a friendly punch on her arm. "There you go again."

Mission 4, Wishworld Observation #4, thought Vega. *Sometimes Wishlings use words the opposite way. For example,* sick.

"Oh, you'll see," said Katie. "She wears a cool outfit every day." She thought for a minute. "I guess I don't really know all that much about her. She kind of keeps to herself. She never invites anyone over. It could be because her mom designs her clothes at home and everything needs to be top secret," she mused. "Or maybe it's because her mom has to travel a lot."

"Oh," said Vega. She started thinking. Maybe Ella's wish was to spend more time with her mother. She wondered how she would make that happen. Maybe she could suggest they take up a hobby together. . . .

Katie was looking at her intently. "I said, where should we drop you off, Vega?"

Vega snapped back to reality. *Uh-oh.* She had no idea what to tell her. Then she had a sudden brainstorm. "Your house?" she suggested. "My mom's at work, so I have some time to kill."

The other girl's face lit up in a smile. "Excellent," she said. "Maybe you could stay for dinner!"

"I'd love to," said Vega.

After a couple more blocks, the car stopped and the driver got out and opened the door for them. They stepped onto the sidewalk under an awning.

"Thank you, Michael," said Katie. "See you tomorrow!"

"Thank you," echoed Vega.

A smiling man in a fancy uniform held the door of the building open for them. "Good evening, Katie," he said.

"Good evening, Henry," she replied.

They walked through the lobby, past a large marble table, on which rested the largest vase of flowers Vega had ever seen. She literally could have taken a dip in it. They stepped into the elevator, where another uniformed man was waiting.

"Hello, Ernest," Katie said, and he nodded, taking the girls straight to the right floor. "Going up!" he said.

Vega followed Katie down a polished hallway to a door. Katie rang the doorbell, which chimed melodiously. A woman, clad in a gray dress with a white apron over it, answered the door.

"Welcome home, Katie," she said.

Katie gave her a quick hug. "Marta, this is my friend Vega. She's going to stay for dinner tonight."

"Very good," Marta said. She nodded and disappeared.

"Is that your mom?" asked Vega curiously.

Katie snorted. "No, my mom doesn't wear a uniform, silly. And I don't call her by her first name, either. That's our housekeeper." She playfully punched Vega in the arm again. "You're so funny!"

My *mom wears a uniform*, thought Vega. She realized she had to start keeping her observations to herself. She wasn't really blending in. In fact, she was starting to stick out like a sore thumb. How soon before her funny comments caught some unwanted attention?

"Want a tour?" asked Katie.

"Sure," said Vega.

The tour took half an hour. They started in the sun-filled living room, which was bigger than the apartment Vega grew up in. They saw the dining room, with a table big enough for fourteen; the huge gleaming kitchen; and at least four bedrooms. Vega lost count. "My mom and dad's room is that way," said Katie, pointing to an unexplored wing of the house. Off a library, filled from floor to ceiling with real paper books, was a balcony that overlooked a huge green rectangle. "That's the park," Katie explained.

Vega nodded. Which park? She wanted to ask, but she knew enough by then not to.

The tour continued: The windowless media room with a huge screen, plush red theater seats, and a popcorn machine. The maid's room. The laundry room. They ended the tour in Katie's enormous bedroom—complete with huge canopy bed, private bathroom, a crafts table, and a gigantic walk-in closet.

Vega's eyes were huge. "My stars," she said.

A bell jangled.

"Dinnertime!" said Katie. The two girls washed their hands and headed back to the dining room. Luckily, Katie waited for Vega, or she would probably have gotten lost trying to find it.

The enormous dining room table was set for two. Vega didn't think twice about that. She had often eaten alone when her mother worked late. She sat at the table, unfolded her napkin, and placed it across her lap.

Just then a lovely woman in a long black dress swept into the room. Her shining blond hair was twisted into a sleek updo. Vega admired the sparkling white crystals she wore around her wrist and neck.

"This is my mother, Mrs. O'Toole," Katie said. "Mom, this is my new friend Vega."

"You look beautiful!" Vega exclaimed.

"She's dressed like this because she's off to a benefit tonight," Katie explained.

"Vega. What a pretty name," said Mrs. O'Toole. "I'm pleased to meet you."

"Pleased to meet you," Vega repeated. What a lovely Wishling expression!

"And what a pretty haircut," Katie's mother said. She took a closer look at Vega's hair. "Look at that! There's a hidden layer of blue underneath in the back!"

"There is?" said Vega, reaching back to touch her hair.

Mrs. O'Toole and Katie laughed the same tinkling laugh. "Your new friend is funny," Mrs. O'Toole said to Katie.

"Tell me about it," said Katie.

Mrs. O'Toole turned to her daughter. "Daddy and I will be out late tonight, so you must listen to Marta. And go to bed when she tells you." She sniffed the air. "Did Marta make lemon meringue pie?" she asked.

Katie gave her mom a strange look. "I don't think so," she said. Then her eyes lit up. "Hey, can Vega sleep over tonight?"

"I'm sure her mother is expecting her," Mrs. O'Toole said worriedly. "And it is a school night. And we've never met, so I can't imagine that her mother would allow—"

"Why don't I stay over tonight?" interrupted Vega. "My mother won't mind."

Katie's mother got a funny look on her face. "Why don't you stay over tonight?" she said. "Your mother won't mind."

Katie looked puzzled, but delight won out over confusion, and she hugged Vega, then her mother. "That's totally dope, Mom!" she said.

"Glad to be so dope," said her mother. "Word."

"Now you're embarrassing me," said Katie.

A man in a white shirt, a black suit, and a black bow tie strode into the room. "Who's embarrassing you?" he asked. "Is it me in my penguin suit?"

He looked dashing, so Vega knew he was kidding. He

introduced himself to Vega, then said to Katie, "I'm getting dragged to another of your mother's charity events. I'd much rather stay home and watch baseball with you!"

Katie grinned. "Tomorrow night, Daddy. The whales need you."

He rumpled her hair. "Tomorrow night it is." He stood up and smiled. "You girls are in for a treat. It smells like Marta made chocolate layer cake!"

After dinner Vega watched as Katie did her homework. Sitting silently as Katie struggled with math was particularly painful for Vega, so she stood, walked to the window, and looked up, searching the night sky. But to her dismay she couldn't see a single star.

There was a scratching sound at the door and Vega whirled around. To her surprise, two enormous furry creatures bounded into the room. Vega took one look and screamed.

Katie looked up and laughed. "Don't be scared. That's just Felix and Oscar. My mother raises Afghan hounds," she explained.

Vega stared at the tall, slender, long-haired creatures. "They're dogs?" she guessed.

Katie laughed. "Well, they're not hamsters," she said.

"They're not?" said Vega.

Katie grinned. "Vega, you are too much. They're my mother's show dogs."

They put on shows? Vega wondered. *What is their talent?* But she wisely kept her thoughts to herself this time.

"They compete in dog shows all over the country," explained Katie. "They are the most spoiled dogs in the city, I swear. They have their own water fountain in the kitchen, their own special shower room, and they eat meals prepared by a doggy chef. You can't make this stuff up."

Vega tentatively held out her hand and one of the dogs licked it. It was kind of gross and kind of cool at the same time. She patted its head and then, emboldened, began to stroke its silky fur. The other dog poked her with its long nose, looking for attention, too.

Katie grinned. "You'll never get rid of them now."

"Katie?" asked Vega.

"Yeah?"

"Does everyone at school live in as big a place as this?"

Katie thought for a moment. "Most of them, I guess," she said. She frowned. "Actually, not everyone. There are some FA kids who live outside the city, in smaller apartments."

"FA kids?" asked Vega.

"Financial aid," Katie explained. "You know. The kids that get scholarships to be able to go to school."

"All schools aren't free?" asked Vega. That was strange. They were on Starland.

"Definitely not," Katie said. "Especially ours!"

That night Vega lay in an impeccably decorated guest room under crisp white sheets and a blanket the color of the early-morning sky and as soft as a baby's skin. She ran over the day's events and her next steps, making a mental list.

1) Make secondary contact with Ella.

2) Get invited over to her house.

3) Determine wish.

4) Make wish come true.

And then she couldn't help adding:

5) Help Leona become happy again.

6) Find Scarlet (and convince her to rejoin band).

7) Check on flowers in botany lab (and hopefully collect on bet!).

8) Try to get along better with Piper.

9) Call Mom back.

As Vega thought of her mom, she pictured her curling up in bed with a good holo-book and some jellyjoobles, her mom's favorite thing to do after a long shift at the hospital. Then Vega got a weird lump in her throat and she had to get up and drink a glass of water. But it didn't help. So to feel better, she closed her eyes and repeated her mantra over and over again:

You are the missing piece of the puzzle.

You are the missing piece of the puzzle.

You are the missing piece of the puzzle.

You are the missing piece of the puzzle.

You are the missing piece of the puzzle.

You are the missing piece of the puzzle.

Until she fell finally fell asleep, a peaceful smile on her face.

CHAPTER
6

"Shouldn't we wait for your parents?" asked Vega as she slathered jam on a delicious-smelling crossed-sant, or at least that's what she thought it was called. Surely this gigantic spread was not for just her and Katie. She popped a fat red berry with little yellow seeds all over it into her mouth and poured herself a glass of freshly squeezed glorange juice.

Or-ange, she corrected herself.

"Oh, no, I'm sure they were up really late last night," explained Katie.

Vega felt another lump rise in her throat as she recalled how her mother had greeted her with a tasty breakfast every morning before she went to school, regardless of how late her mom had worked the night before.

It was pleasant to ride to school in the luxurious car and have the door opened for them, like they were famous or something. The girls walked up the stone steps and Vega followed Katie into her classroom. She walked right up to the teacher and introduced herself as she had been instructed. "Hello, I am Vega, the new student in your class," she told her teacher, Ms. McKenney, a woman with green eyes, auburn hair, and an easy grin.

It worked like a charm. And it made her happy when Ms. McKenney said that the room smelled like coconut layer cake.

Vega got settled at her new desk and waited patiently for her Wisher to appear. She was starting to get anxious when Ms. McKenney shut the door and started the morning's attendance and Ella still hadn't arrived. Finally, to Vega's relief, there was a knock on the door. Ms. McKenney opened it. "Thanks for joining us!" she said to the red-faced girl. She said it kindly, but Ella looked miserable as she slunk to her seat behind Katie.

"Your driver got stuck in traffic?" Katie asked sympathetically.

Ella raised her eyebrows. "Yeah, something like that," she muttered.

Vega was not a fashionista; she was the furthest thing from it, actually, as she preferred function over form at all times. But once again she had to admire Ella's outfit choice: a black cape with a hood over a pair of jeans with artfully arranged multicolored patches and a pair of distressed ankle boots. She could see Scarlet (poor Scarlet) wearing that exact same cape. The arms, she decided as she watched, looked very much like bat wings. Yes, Scarlet would be all over that cape in an instant. Ella removed the cape and hung it over the back of her seat, revealing the sparkly maroon shrug she had completed in Knitting Club the day before.

As the morning progressed, Vega was disappointed to discover that there were no clues to be had about Ella's wish. The girl seemed to have it all—smarts (she finished a math problem everyone else but Vega, of course, was struggling with), admirers (three girls told her they were going to join the Knitting Club, too, so they could learn how to knit a shrug just like hers), and style. What could Ella want that she didn't have? Vega wondered. The only possible lead she had at the moment was Ella's busy designer mom. She'd have to look into that, and soon.

The bell rang for lunch and the students stood at their desks, putting books and papers and writing utensils into their backpacks. "Class! Class!" shouted Ms.

McKenney. "Don't forget that Bring Your Parent to School Day is coming up on Friday. There are still some parents we haven't heard from, so please have them fill out the slip and return it to me as soon as you are able. We would like all our parents to participate if possible!"

She indicated a list pinned to the bulletin board. Vega stole a glance at the list on her way out the door. Ella's name was not on it. She got a shiver of excitement and wondered: *Could this be my first clue?*

She could be on to something. She watched with interest as Katie turned and spoke briefly with Ella.

Ella disappeared into the surge of students in the hallway, and Vega hurried to catch up with Katie. "What did you say to Ella?" she asked.

"Oh, I just told her how excited I am to meet her mom," she said.

"And what did Ella say?" Vega asked.

"She said she doesn't think it's going to happen. Her mom is in Paris and she doesn't think she'll be back in time," Katie said, frowning. She crossed her fingers. "Fingers crossed she can make it!"

Vega headed to the cafeteria in search of Ella. She couldn't find her anywhere, and finally her hunger got the better of her and she got into the lunch line behind some other students. The line was long, and she used the opportunity to try to discover her special talent. She ran down a mental list. It wasn't levitation or making time stand still (or speed up). She turned to the girl behind her and tried out mind reading (nothing). She stared at a cookie, willing it to disappear. Nothing. Finally, it was her turn to order her lunch. She glanced up at all the unfamiliar menu items. Pizza. Hamburgers. Chicken tenders. Tomato soup. Grilled cheese. Suddenly, she had an idea. She surreptitiously tapped her elbows together three times for luck. "I'll have a slice of pizza please," she told the woman pleasantly. Then she thought, *Give me a grilled cheese. Give me a grilled cheese. Give me a grilled cheese.*

The woman reached for the pizza, then stopped, a puzzled look on her face. Before Vega's delighted eyes, she shook her head, picked up a toasted sandwich, and handed it to Vega uncertainly.

"Thank you so much!" Vega said effusively. Now she was certain! Her star talent was mind control! This was a tough one because she knew that she couldn't use this talent directly on her Wisher. So she wasn't sure exactly how she was going to use it, but she was certainly glad to have the knowledge in her back pocket.

She grabbed some napkins (paper, which was odd to her) and then stood uncertainly, balancing her tray as she scanned the room, looking for a familiar face. She smiled when she spotted Katie. Even better, there was an empty seat at her table. Vega headed over.

"Vega!" said Katie. "Sit down. You remember Luna, Callie, and Lila from class?"

The girls smiled at her and Vega nodded back, although she had been so focused on Ella, she hadn't noticed any of the other students.

Vega sat and took a bite of her grilled cheese sandwich. She was pleasantly surprised by how tasty it was. She chewed and swallowed. "So what happens on Bring Your Parents to School Day?" she asked.

"Oh, parents come in and talk to the students about their jobs," Katie explained.

"Are your parents coming in?" Vega asked.

"My dad is supposed to come in and talk about derivatives," she said. "I love my dad to death but . . ." She gave a dramatic jaw-cracking yawn. "Will either of your parents be able to come?"

Vega's eyes widened. "Oh, I don't think so," she said. "They're, um, away." That certainly wasn't a lie. They were both away from her at the moment; that was for sure. Vega's dad even more so, ever since she was three staryears old. He visited her sporadically and sent her a Bright Day gift every staryear, but he had a new family now in Light City, and every Bright Day she got a staryear older, but his gifts did not. It was like she was five staryears old permanently, in his mind. Vega couldn't throw the gifts away, as inappropriate as they were, and she kept them in the bottom drawer of her dresser. She rarely opened the drawer; it made her very sad to look at them.

The rest of the girls at the table started talking excitedly about who would be the most interesting parent. One girl's mother was a famous actress. Another girl's father had written a best-selling book. Another girl's mother was something called a plastic surgeon, which seemed like it could be quite interesting, as some Wishlings apparently liked to alter their looks. That thought was quite foreign to Vega, because every Starling was innately proud of his or her unique appearance.

Katie grinned. "I hope Ella's mom comes in. I want to ask her where she gets her inspiration from."

"That's right," said another girl. "I mean, her designs are to die for. Ella always looks so good!"

Vega had a free period after lunch, so she headed to the library to wander through the stacks of those paper books Sage and Libby had told her about. She smiled when she stepped inside. The room had floor-to-ceiling windows and a balcony, and everywhere she looked were books, books, and more books, in all colors of the rainbow and all shapes and sizes. Some had hard covers and some had soft covers. Some had the sharp smell of a just-printed page and others had crumbly pages and the odor of history and decay. She wandered through the stacks, pulling out titles and leafing through them. She reached for an extra-large book, called *Guinness World Records*, and was staring with fascination at the picture on the cover—a photo of a man with hundreds of smoking sticks shoved into his mouth—when she looked up and realized that the empty space allowed her to see through the stack to the other side. And there stood Ella!

The girl was stock-still, her fingers crossed and her eyes screwed tightly shut. Could she be . . . could she be wishing? Vega's heart began to race. She whipped out her Star-Zap and pressed the holo-vid button. An actual Wisher in the act of wishing! Everyone would want to see this! "I'm going to try again," she heard Ella whisper. She screwed her eyes shut and crossed her fingers. "I wish this lie of mine would just go away!"

A sudden electric jolt ran through Vega and she dropped her Star-Zap with a clatter. "*Starf!*" she cried.

When Vega straightened up, her Star-Zap in hand, Ella was standing right next to her, glowering. "Were you *spying* on me?" she demanded.

Vega held out her hands to Ella. "Don't be mad at me," she implored. "I can help you! Just tell me—what do you wish you hadn't lied about?"

Ella stared at Vega, furious. "You want to know what I really wish?" she whispered harshly. "I wish that you would leave me alone. Do you think you can help me with that?"

CHAPTER
7

The entire rest of the day, Vega got the silent treatment from Ella. And everybody noticed.

Katie went up to Vega as they made their way to gym class. "What did you say to Ella?" she asked. "Whoa, you are totally getting frozen out."

That was a good way to describe it, Vega thought. There was a definite chill in the air anytime Ella was around. Vega didn't know what to do. Her Countdown Clock told her she had twenty-one starhours to grant the wish. She felt like a failure. She was definitely the first Star Darling whose Wisher wouldn't acknowledge her existence.

In the locker room, Vega was handed a uniform that was tight in the places it should have been baggy and baggy in the places it should have been tight.

"Oh, boy," Katie said when Vega walked into the gym. "That's unfortunate."

Vega shrugged. She had way bigger problems than an ill-fitting gym uniform. "Do you think we'll play lodge-ball?" she asked Katie, remembering the game that Sage had told her about witnessing her Wisher play during her mission. "Maybe Ella and I will be on the same team."

Katie chortled. "Oh, Vega, you're so funny," she said. "And it's not just that ridiculous uniform. Lodgeball!" The gym teacher stood in front of the room, a whistle around her neck. "Today we start our lessons in square dancing," she announced.

Up went a chorus of groans, which the gym teacher ignored. "Square dancing is a type of folk dance," she went on. "Please break up into groups of eight and form a square, two partners on each side."

Katie grabbed Vega's hand and together they formed one side of a square. Vega noticed with disappointment that Ella positioned herself as far away from Vega as she could while still remaining in the gymnasium. She shook her head. How was she going to fix this?

Vega turned to Katie. "What's so bad about square dancing?" she asked.

"You'll see," replied Katie grimly.

But Vega didn't see. It turned out she absolutely loved square dancing. It might have been the orderly way everyone moved. It might have been the sheer novelty of it. Or it might have been the opportunity she had to promenade, do-si-do, and swing with seven different people. Because every time she promenaded, do-si-doed, swung her partner, or allemanded, she got to chat with someone else.

"So tell me about Ella," she said under her breath as she promenaded with a curly-headed girl named Grace.

"Oh, she's nice," Grace said. "She's got great style."

When Vega bowed to her side, she asked a blond girl, "Have you ever been to Ella's house?"

"Never," was the answer. "She never invites any-one over." She lowered her voice. "I think it must be because her mom has some secret designs lying around the house or something. The fashion industry can be cutthroat!"

"Now everybody swing," called the teacher, and Vega found out about every trend Ella had started as she linked arms and swung around with each dancer. Arm warmers. Cat-eye glasses. Two different-colored socks. Mismatched earrings. Paint-speckled shoes. "This," said a girl, holding up a necklace with a brightly painted key on it. "We all wear them now, just like Ella," she explained.

Just then a shiver went down Vega's spine and her skin began to tingle. It was subtle, but it had to be a sign, didn't it? She turned to grin at Ella, across the gym, who glowered back at her. Did she know Vega was talking about her? Vega was pretty sure she had figured out what Ella's lie was. Now she just had to talk to Ella and convince the other girl to let her help fix it. This was going to be a piece of pie. She smiled smugly, mentally congratulating herself for remembering the Wishling phrase that Sage had shared with everyone.

Back in the classroom, Vega received an unexpected opportunity from Ms. McKenney. "Class," the teacher announced, "I want you to pair up to do your writing homework tonight. Your assignment is to interview a classmate with these questions." She held up a sheaf of papers and began handing them out.

"Katie, you're paired with Ivy," she said. "Jill and Maya, please take turns interviewing each other."

Vega saw her chance. She closed her eyes and concentrated. This was going to take an awful lot of her wish energy reserve, so she hoped it would work.

"Ella, you are paired with . . . Lu . . . Lu . . . Lu . . ." She clearly wanted to say a particular name, but it wouldn't come out. "Vega," she finally said.

It had worked! The grin on Vega's face was as intense as Ella's grimace. Maybe even more so.

★

Vega leaned her back against the locker next to Ella's. Ella was aggressively shoving books into her backpack and trying to ignore Vega. But the Starling was fully determined to use this opportunity to her advantage.

"So shall we head to your house?" Vega suggested hopefully.

Ella looked up suddenly, and Vega saw a flash of something in her eyes—anger, or could it be panic? But the girl smoothly said, "Oh, they're polishing our marble entryway today. Let's go to your house instead."

Vega actually did panic. "I . . . um . . . my . . . can't," was all she managed to say.

Ella had the good grace not to laugh at Vega's awkwardness. "Okay then, let's go to the Munch Box," she said, narrowing her eyes at Vega. "Let's get this over with."

The two girls left the school in silence and headed down the steps together. Ella led Vega down the block to a friendly little coffee shop with cozy booths and a counter with funny round seats that appeared to be bolted to the floor. The two girls settled into a booth. Ella started rummaging through her bag. She pulled out a mirror, a wallet, and a small paperback book before she found what she was looking for—a notebook and a purple pen.

Vega stared at the book. "Is that a book of crosswords?" she asked excitedly.

"It is," said Ella. "I do them on the subway." Then she got a horrified look on her face and barked out a laugh. "That was a joke! As if I ever take the subway! I do it in the car when my driver takes me to school."

"What's the subway?" asked Vega. *Starf!* she thought. *Maybe she'll realize I'm not a Wishling!*

But Ella grinned and reached over to give her a friendly punch in the arm. "Right? Nobody who goes to George Robert Prep actually takes the subway!"

Ella picked up a menu and began flipping through it. "I'm getting a hot fudge sundae with chocolate ice cream," she said decidedly.

The menu was so thick and jam-packed with unfamiliar food choices that Vega didn't know where to begin. Chops! Specials! Breakfast served all day! What in the world was a jelly omelet? Or a gyro? Vega was totally overwhelmed, so she simply said, "Me too." She hoped she would like it.

Shortly afterward she discovered that she most certainly did. The sundae, a tantalizing mountain of round scoops of brown, slathered with a thick dark brown sauce, was placed in front of her. A fluffy crown of white and a bright red fruit with a stem sat on top. It looked amazing. Vega licked her lips in anticipation.

"Let's dig in," said Ella, brandishing a long spoon.

The sundae was simply perfection in a chilly metal cup—a lip-smackingly delicious combination of creamy, sweet coldness and warm goodness in every bite. The white fluffy cream was sweet and as light as air. Vega was in heaven. She made a mental note: *Bring a hot fudge sundae home for Tessa.*

While they ate, Vega pulled the list of questions out of her backpack. She gave the stuffed blue star keychain a squeeze for luck. "Do you mind if I go first?" she asked Ella.

"Shoot," said Ella.

"What?" asked Vega, totally confused.

Ella laughed. "Go ahead."

"What is your greatest joy?" Vega asked her.

Ella bit her lip and stared into space. "I guess it's

being creative," she said slowly. "Like I'll show up for school in paint-splattered shoes or two different-colored socks, and the day after, one girl is doing it, and then the next week it's five girls, and soon it's a trend in the entire school. Even the older girls are copying my style."

Vega wrote that all down. It was fun to write in a paper notebook with a writing utensil—very old-fashioned and extremely satisfying.

"What is your biggest dream for the future?" was the next question.

Vega looked up. Ella's cheeks were flushed and she looked excited. It was the first time Vega had seen her look relaxed and unguarded.

"I'm going to be a fashion designer," she said. "I'm going to create new fashions that no one has ever seen before. I'm going to come up with something people will be talking about forever, like the jumpsuit or the maxi dress."

"Just like your mom," said Vega.

Ella looked away. "Yeah, just like my mom."

"And last but not least, what is your biggest fear?"

Ella stared into the distance. She opened her mouth, then closed it. "Um, my biggest fear is that everyone . . ."

Vega leaned forward. "Yes?"

"That everyone . . ." she thought for a moment and frowned. "That everyone . . . um, won't like my fashions," she concluded.

"That's it?" asked Vega.

"That's it," Ella said firmly. "Now your turn."

Vega, with some creative thinking and some serious self-editing, was able to answer the questions. She spoke about her dream of being a top student and her love of puzzles of all kinds. And all of a sudden she found herself explaining that her biggest fear was not making her mother proud of her, after she had worked so hard to provide for Vega. She had never put those thoughts into words, and she grew teary as she said them. When she looked up, she saw that Ella looked a bit tearful, too.

The two girls smiled at each other. "That was great," said Ella. "I really learned a lot about you today."

"Me too," said Vega. "You're a really interesting person."

Ella checked her watch. "All right, well, I guess I had better go," she said reluctantly.

"Oh, is your driver waiting?" Vega asked.

Ella got a funny look on her face, then nodded. "Yes, my driver is waiting. That's right." She grabbed the key pendant that hung around her neck, as if she was checking that it was there.

It's now or never, Vega thought. "I know what your lie is," she blurted out.

Ella bit her lip. "You do?" She didn't look angry anymore, just sad and embarrassed.

"Your mom isn't really in Paris," Vega said.

Ella nodded. She looked ashamed but almost relieved.

"You don't want her to come in for Bring Your Parents to School Day because you don't want the other girls to pester her into making them fashions. You want to keep her creations all to yourself!" Vega concluded.

Ella stared at Vega, who sat back in the booth, feeling triumphant.

Then Ella stood up. "You couldn't have it any more wrong if you tried," she said. She threw some money on the table and stormed out of the coffee shop, the bell over the door tinkling cheerfully and adding a merry note to a decidedly unpleasant parting.

Vega watched her go, her heart sinking. She suddenly felt tired and cranky. She decided she would head to the school roof, where she would pitch her invisible tent. She glanced at her Star-Zap and accessed the Countdown Clock. Nineteen starhours and counting. *Starf!* She was running out of time. If she didn't have Ella's wish granted by the next day at noon, Leona wasn't going to be the only Star Darling who didn't collect any wish energy!

CHAPTER
8

"What are you doing here?" Vega asked.

When she had opened the flaps of her tent the next morning, she was shocked to see Clover standing at the edge of the roof, admiring the view.

Clover turned around, raised her eyebrow, and smirked at Vega. Her look said, *You know why I'm here.*

"I guess I already know," said Vega with a sigh. "My mission is dangerously close to failing?"

"Your mission is dangerously close to failing," confirmed Clover. She walked over to the tent, her arms folded tightly across her chest. "Spill it."

So Vega did.

"There's only one thing to do," said Clover. "You've got to find her, figure out what she actually *did* lie about, and fix it, all in"—she checked Vega's Countdown Clock—"four starhours."

"I think I can do it," said Vega. "I just need to get her alone. We started to have a connection yesterday. . . ."

"Well, let's find her right away," said Clover. "You just have to keep thinking. Is there a detail that you missed . . . a small clue that will help us figure it all out?"

The two girls left the roof and headed downstairs. They walked down the hallway to Ms. McKenney's classroom. When they got there, it was crowded with students and their parents, all of them buzzing with excitement. A doctor in a white lab coat was wheeling a human skeleton into the room. A book editor arrived with a stack of books to hand out. "Signed by the author!" bragged Luna.

"Hi, Vega," said Katie's dad. He took the stack of charts from under his arm and placed it on Katie's desk.

"This is going to be deadly," whispered Katie. "I can't watch!"

Vega grabbed her arm. "Where's Ella?" she asked.

"I overheard Ms. McKenney saying she wasn't coming in today," answered Katie. "I guess her mom didn't come back from Paris after all. What a disappointment."

Vega just stared at her. That was way more than a disappointment. That was a disaster!

Just then Callie and her mother rushed into the classroom. Callie's mom, who ran a modeling agency, was carrying a big shiny box filled with head shots. Callie looked repulsed. "You'll never believe it," she said. "We couldn't get a cab, so we had to take the *subway*."

"Ewwwww," said Lila. "My mother never lets me take the subway."

The subway . . . the subway . . . Why did that seem so familiar? All of a sudden Vega remembered her and Ella's words. "Is that a book of crosswords?" Vega had asked. And Ella had said, "It is. I do them on the subway."

And Ella's mom had not gone to Paris. . . . And the key she wore around her neck . . . It wasn't the latest trend in necklaces—it was her house key! Her distressed boots? Well, it was quite possible they were just old.

"Oh, my stars," said Vega. "I had it all wrong. It's so simple. I'm such an idiot."

Clover grinned and opened her mouth as if she was about to say something.

"Don't you dare agree with me!" said Vega.

Clover just smiled.

"I'll explain it all on the way to Ella's house," said Vega. "But first I've got to find out where she lives!"

All she had to say was "You forgot to tell me what Ella's address is," to the school secretary, who handed it right over, no questions asked. Oh . . . there was *one*. It was "Are they serving German chocolate cake in the cafeteria today?"

Clover laughed. "So it's true! We do smell like dessert!"

Vega looked down. Her wish energy was depleted. She stared at the address in her hand. There was no way around it. They were going to have to take the dreaded subway to get there.

"I don't know what everyone is freaking out about," said Clover as they sat in the subway car. The train rocked and shimmied as it sped through the underground tunnels.

"It gets you where you want to go pretty fast, it doesn't cost a lot, and it provides free entertainment," said Vega, listing the subway pros on her fingers. She pointed to a young man who had just finished playing his guitar and was walking through the car, offering people money from his hat.

"Thank you," she said, removing one Wishling dollar. That was certainly generous of him!

He had a funny look on his face, but then he laughed. "Um, you're welcome," he said.

"So spill the stars," said Clover, crossing her arms.

"I put it all together," said Vega. "She takes the subway. She lives outside the city. She said her mother was not in Paris. Katie told me that some students at George Robert aren't as wealthy as the others. Some kids get financial aid because the school costs so much. I'm pretty sure Ella's lie was that she told everyone that her mother is a successful fashion designer. I think maybe business isn't going very well and she doesn't want everyone to find out about it, because it would embarrass her mom."

The train emerged from the tunnel onto an elevated track.

Clover frowned. "You really think that's it? So what's her wish then?"

Vega thought hard for a moment. "She wishes that . . . she never said that about her mom?" Her brow furrowed. "But that's an impossible wish." She sighed. "This is all very confusing. I'm not sure how to fix this and time is running out." She looked down at her Star-Zap. "And this is our stop."

They exited the train car and found themselves on an open-air platform with a pretty mosaic sign. They headed downstairs, crossed a large boulevard, and headed straight down the block. There were fewer trees in that neighborhood and not as many flowers. Not as many people, either. Little Wishlings ran down the street and rode their tricycles while their caretakers watched, smiling.

Finally, they reached Ella's building—a solid brick fortress at the end of the block. Vega could see the tall skyscrapers of the city in the distance. Against the bright blue sky and soft fluffy clouds drifting by, it looked magical, like a fairy-tale city.

Vega used the last grains of her wish energy to push open the locked door. She and Clover rode the elevator in silence. They rang the buzzer for 6F.

No answer.

"I can't believe it!" said Vega. "Where is she? What are we going to do?"

The door swung open. Ella stood there, looking furious. "What are you doing here?" She looked at Clover. "And who is this?" she asked.

"This is my friend Clover," said Vega.

"Pleased to meet you," said Ella. "Nice boots."

"Thanks," said Clover, glancing down at her soft-brown fringed footwear.

Ella turned back to Vega, her mouth set in a thin, hard line. "Now get out of here," she said. "My mother is home. I don't want her to know what happened. She might think I'm embarrassed of her and that would kill me."

"I think I can help you," said Vega.

"No one can help me," retorted Ella. "I've gotten myself into this stupid mess and I don't know how to get out."

"You have to trust me," Vega said. "I'm here to help you." She smiled at Ella. "Sometimes when I'm feeling lost I say a special phrase to myself. I call it my mantra. And it helps me, it gives me strength. Do you want to say it with me?"

Ella rolled her eyes. But she gave a small smile and shrugged. "Sure," she said. "I've got nothing to lose."

Vega grasped Ella's hands in hers and recited her mantra: "You are the missing piece of the puzzle."

Ella gasped and stepped back. "How did you know?"

"I . . . um. . . ." Vega stammered. How did she know what?

Ella grabbed Vega's hand and pulled her inside the apartment. Clover was right behind her. The apartment was spotless, very cozy, and welcoming.

The small foyer had a tiny hand-painted table and a

mosaic-framed mirror. In the living room was a massive red-and-gold-striped couch, a festive rug, and an antique chandelier hanging from the ceiling. The hallway that led to the kitchen and bedrooms had a dining room table and a china cabinet filled with vintage china in many different patterns. The sunny kitchen had fun antique signs advertising SARSAPARILLA: 5 CENTS A GLASS and FRESH EGGS. Ella took the girls into her neat bedroom, which had a stunning view of the city skyline.

"What a lovely place," said Vega.

"Thanks," said Ella. "On weekends my mom and I go to flea markets and thrift stores. We love to decorate."

Then her face hardened. "I got myself into a real mess," she said. "When I first got the scholarship to the school I was excited, but a little nervous that I wouldn't fit in. But I decided I was going to just tell the truth. Then I met Katie and I really liked her. She asked what my parents did and I told her that my mother was a housekeeper for a famous fashion designer, and I guess Katie only heard the 'famous fashion designer' part. She told everyone, and I don't know, I guess I liked the way it sounded. People were suddenly really nice to me. And then instead of correcting them, I let it go."

Vega was confused. "Wait, so then who makes all your great clothes?"

Ella smiled and shrugged. And there in the corner was the answer—a sewing machine and a dress form with a half-made skirt on it.

"You really are the missing piece of the puzzle!" said Vega.

"Now you know," said Ella. "I take old castaway clothes that my mother's employer gives her and stuff I find at vintage stores and I redesign them into clothes for me." She shook her head. "The girls at school are going to be angry when they realize that the clothes they were gushing over aren't couture—just stuff I sewed together in my bedroom." She looked at the ground. "Now I'll be the laughingstock of the school."

"You've got it all wrong, Ella," said Vega. "The girls in school are going to be lining up to take lessons from you. It's going to make your lie go away."

"Really?" said Ella.

"Really," said Vega. "You just have to trust me."

CHAPTER
9

Vega had to convince the principal that George Robert Prep needed a forty-eighth club—Sewing and Fashion. She didn't want to do it the forceful way; she really wanted to convince the woman that it was a good idea, for Ella's sake. She told the principal the whole story, trying hard not to check her watch as she did it. There were mere starmins left.

"So all we need to do is borrow the PA system," said Vega. "Make a quick announcement. Two starm—I mean minutes, tops."

"This is highly irregular," said the principal. She sighed. "But I'll allow it." She headed back to her office. And as the door closed, Vega heard the principal ask her secretary, "Just who is that girl again?"

Ella cleared her throat. Her hand shook as she read the announcement that the three girls had cobbled together on the ride back to the city. "Hello, everyone. Ella Silverstone here. I have an exciting announcement to make. I know you all thought that my mother was the designer behind all my fashions, but it really was me!" She made a face like she was going to be sick, then soldiered on. "And guess what? I'm starting a new after-school club called Designing with Ella. We'll learn how to take old articles of clothing and transform them into fashions that are completely unique and one of a kind. I have room for twenty students and it is first come, first served. See you this afternoon in room 228."

She shut off the intercom. "First come, first served," she said with a shudder. "Why did I say that?"

The end-of-the-day bell rang and the three girls could hear the students running down the hallways, anxious to get outside. "Do you think anyone is going to show up?" Ella asked.

"I do," said Vega. *I hope*, she thought.

They stood, and Vega and Clover each picked up a box filled with old clothing and fabric scraps Ella had brought. Ella hoisted her sewing machine and they headed up the stairs.

The woman with the clipboard sat behind the table. She looked at them expectantly.

"We're going to Designing with Ella," said Vega.

"Never heard of it," said the woman.

"It's in room 228," said Ella. "It's a new club."

The woman waved them through.

Standing in front of the door, Ella took a deep breath. Then she opened the door.

"Oh," she said softly.

Vega peeked over her shoulder. The room was full of girls all eager to join Ella's club.

"Pick me, pick me!" a girl said. "I love fashion."

"Ella!" said another. "I loaned you my history notes last week, you owe me one!"

Ella looked around the room, a grin spreading across her face.

"Ella!" Luna shouted. "Is your mom coming today?"

Ella took a deep breath. "No," she said. "She isn't coming. I have to tell you the truth. My mom actually isn't a fashion designer. I made all the clothes myself."

Katie pushed to the front of the room. "Who cares?" she said. "That doesn't matter. All we want is to make clothes just like you."

"That's right!" said Luna. "So, am I in?"

Vega gasped as an incredible shower of multicolored sparkles rose from Ella and bounced around the room. She turned and caught Clover's shocked expression. "It's so beautiful!" she breathed. Ella's wish—for her lie to go away—had come true.

Ella turned to Vega and Clover. She looked stunned, tearful, and very happy, all at the same time. "Thank you," she said. "I can't believe it. My wish has come true."

"Believe it," said Vega.

CHAPTER
10

Vega stood in front of Lady Stella's office door, collecting herself. She tried to make her face look serious, but she was so proud and so excited that it was impossible to stop smiling. Mindful of Leona's feelings, she managed to dim the wattage of her grin, at least a little bit. Nope, there it was again.

Her mission had not been easy. She had misinterpreted it and had a difficult time figuring it out. She had almost completely alienated her Wisher. She was especially grateful to Clover. She knew she wouldn't have collected the wish energy without her help.

Just as she raised her hand to knock on the door, she reached into her pocket and stole a glance at her

Star-Zap. The red star around the image of her mother's face was still there, a visible reminder of what a terrible daughter she had been. She resolved to call her mother on the way back to the dorm that evening. She'd make a plan for a visit home for certain.

Vega placed the Star-Zap back in her pocket, adjusted her collar, and knocked on the door. It slid open. The moment she stepped into the room, everyone jumped to their feet and started cheering. She stood there, grinning and feeling proud, slightly embarrassed, and totally wonderful. She'd had no idea that a standing ovation could feel quite so good. Even Leona was cheering.

When the excitement died down, Lady Stella called Vega forward and handed her the orb. It felt warm and substantial in her hand, and she liked the weight of it. It started to glow so brightly Vega wished she had on her safety starglasses. Then, before her eyes, it began to transform into a flower: first a stem sprouted; then the orb itself was surrounded with petals—deep blue giving way to icy blue. "It's a bluebubble," Vega breathed. "My favorite flower of all." Glowing points of light orbited the blossom. "The petals open and close so regularly you can use it to tell time," she told the others proudly.

Vega was even more delighted when her Power Crystal, a gorgeous queezle, emerged. It was stunning!

Sparkling crystalline blue nuggets were held together by their own internal magnetic force. Vega held it up and took a closer look. "Is it . . . is it Eleanor's Equation?" she asked Lady Stella in disbelief.

The headmistress nodded in affirmation. "Yes," she said. She turned to the others. "The nuggets may seem to be arranged chaotically," she explained. "But they actually represent a precise mathematical equation."

Lady Stella took the flower, which was beginning to transform into a Silver Blossom, and placed it on her desk.

Clover shook her head. "I was only there to help," she said. But Vega could tell that she was pleased.

To her chagrin, Vega noticed that Leona looked away and Ophelia gave her a quick, supportive hug. This couldn't be easy on her.

Just then Vega remembered something. She had made a quick stop at the diner just before she left for home. "Tessa, don't think I wasn't listening," she said. "I brought you back something chocolate—a hot fudge sundae!"

Tessa clapped her hands. "Startastic!" she said.

Vega reached into her backpack, pulled out the paper bag, and handed it to Tessa. Everyone oohed as it made a rustling sound. Licking her lips in anticipation, Tessa reached in and pulled out the container and a pink plastic spoon. Libby grabbed for it, admiring the color.

Tessa lifted the lid. "Ta-da!" she said.

Everyone stared at the sloppy brown mess inside.

"You brought me soup?" Tessa asked.

"Now you know," Lady Stella said with a tinkling laugh. "Wishling food . . . often requires refrigeration!"

Vega laughed. "Here's my last Wishworld observation—ice cream melts!"

Vega pressed the END HOLO-CALL button on her Star-Zap. Why wasn't her mother answering? Was she mad at Vega for taking so long to call back? That seemed very unlike her. But Vega still felt a tiny bit worried. Her mission had opened her eyes to a lot of things, including the importance of being proud of where you came from. She wanted to call her mom and hear her voice and tell her she loved her and was grateful for all the sacrifices she had made. Ella had helped Vega see all that, and she felt that the mission had been eye-opening for them both.

She yawned. She was so sleepy! Traveling to Wishworld and granting a Wisher's wish had certainly taken a lot of energy out of her! She didn't feel like moving her feet, so she willed the Cosmic Transporter to pick up the pace. The sooner she was under the covers, the better. It didn't work, of course.

It seemed like the slowest journey to her dorm room ever. Finally, she stood in front of her door and placed her hand on the scanner. "Welcome home, Vega," said the Bot-Bot voice. "And congratulations on a job well done!"

"Star salutations," Vega said automatically. She stepped inside the dark room and stopped in her tracks. She had been away only a couple of stardays, but she suddenly realized how homesick she had been. She placed her hand on her pride and joy—a large, beautiful secretary desk that had belonged to her great-grandmother on her mother's side. It had a curved top that rolled up and down like a dream (despite its age) and dozens of perfectly labeled drawers and nooks inside. Vega's mother told her that her great-grandmother had been just as organized and precise as she.

She placed her Star-Zap on top of the desk.

"You remind me so much of her sometimes," said someone with a familiar voice. Vega spun around. The room seemed empty. Was she hearing things?

She gasped as a figure stepped out of the shadows. Vega recognized who it was immediately and raced across

the room, then fell into outstretched arms. She inhaled
the comforting and oh-so-familiar smell of gossamer
perfume, boingtree needles, and hospital disinfectant.

"Oh, Mama," she said. "I'm so happy to see you. But
how . . ."

"Piper called me and suggested I come for a visit,"
she said. "And I'm so glad she did. I've missed you so
much, starshine."

Tears filled Vega's eyes as she heard her childhood
nickname. She concentrated her wish manipulation
energy and the light switched on. She looked up and saw
the tiny crinkles around her mother's violet eyes, the
curve of her chin, her striking cheekbones. Her mother's
thin, graceful hands, equally capable of holding a child's
hand and lifting a heavy patient, stroked her blue hair.
That was what Vega had been missing. The empty space
she had been feeling was filled.

Vega lay in bed, content. Her mission had been a resound-
ing success, both for her and for her Wisher. She and her
mom had parted with big hugs and a plan to spend the
upcoming holiday relaxing and playing games together.
She sighed with happiness.

Just then her Star-Zap buzzed. She was so sleepy she

considered ignoring it, but her curiosity got the better of her and she reached out for it.

Sure it had been strange to have to say "Not much" when her mother had asked her what she had been up to lately. Only the most incredible adventure of her entire life, that's all! And it had been so tempting to brag (a little) about how she had saved her Wish Mission, just in the nick of time. To say nothing about the Wish Blossom and Power Crystal she had just received. It had been hard to dim the wattage of her huge smile when that happened, but she managed to tone it down a bit, for Leona's sake. Vega would have liked nothing better than to have been able to pull the Power Crystal out of her bag and show it to her mother. She sighed. Maybe someday . . . She pressed a button and a holo-text appeared in front of her.

She read it, read it again, and then gasped. Piper murmured in her sleep but didn't wake up. Vega read the holo-text again to make sure she wasn't mistaken. But there it was, clear as day: MEET ME IN THE HEDGE MAZE TOMORROW. WE NEED TO TALK. SCARLET.

Glossary

Age of Fulfillment: The age when a Starling is considered mature enough to begin to study wish granting.

Astromuffins: Baked breakfast treat.

Bad Wish Orbs: Orbs that are the result of bad or selfish wishes made on Wishworld. These grow dark and warped and are quickly sent to the Negative Energy Facility.

Bloombug: A purple-and-pink-spotted bug that goes wild during the full moon in warm weather.

Bluebeezel: Delicate bright blue flowers that emit a scent that only glitterbees can detect.

Bluebubble: Vega's Wish Blossom. Deep blue gives way to icy blue in the petals of this compact illuminated flower. Glowing points of light illuminate the blossom. Its petals open and close with such regularity that you can set it to tell time.

Boingtree: A shrublike tree with tickly aromatic needles.

Bot-Bot: A Starland robot. There are Bot-Bot guards, waiters, deliverers, and guides on Starland.

Bright Day: The date a Starling is born, celebrated each year like Wishling birthdays.

Calliope: A glittery yellow flower with ruffly petals and a magenta center.

Callistola: A tiny green bell-like flower that emits a faint tinkling sound when shaken. They smell a lot like ripe ozziefruit.

Celestial Café: Starling Academy's outstanding cafeteria.

Cocomoon: A sweet and creamy fruit with an iridescent glow.

Cosmic Transporter: The moving sidewalk system that transports students through dorms and across the Starling Academy campus.

Countdown Clock: A timing device on a Starling's Star-Zap. It lets them know how much time is left on a Wish Mission, which coincides with when the Wish Orb will fade.

Crystal Mountains: The most beautiful mountains on Starland. They are located across the lake from Starling Academy.

Cyber Journal: Where the Star Darlings record their Wishworld observations.

Cycle of Life: A Starling's life span. When Starlings die, they are said to have "completed their Cycle of Life."

Dododay: The third day of the starweek. The days in order are Sweetday, Shineday, Dododay, Yumday, Lunarday, Bopday, Reliquaday, and Babsday. (Starlandians have a three-day weekend every starweek.)

Double starweek: Sixteen stardays.

Flash Vertical Mover: A mode of transportation similar to a Wishling elevator, only superfast.

Florafierce: Glowing stardust rises from the middle of this flower's fiery red petals.

Flutterfocus: A Starland creature similar to a Wishworld butterfly but with illuminated wings.

Galliope: A sparkly Starland creature similar to a Wishworld horse.

Garble greens: A Starland vegetable similar to spinach.

Glion: A gentle Starland creature similar in appearance to a Wishworld lion, but with a multicolored glowing mane.

Glitterbees: Blue-and-orange-striped bugs that pollinate Starland flowers and produce a sweet substance called gossamer.

Globerbeem: Large, friendly lightning bug–type insects that lay eggs.

Glorange: A glowing orange fruit. Its juice is often enjoyed at breakfast time.

Glowin' Glions: Starling Academy's champion E-ball team.

Good Wish Orbs: Orbs that are the result of positive wishes made on Wishworld. They are planted in Wish-Houses.

Gossamer: A sweet and fragrant liquid made by glitterbees, often used in baking.

Halo Hall: The building where Starling Academy classes are held.

Holo–diary: A book used for jotting down thoughts and feelings that is a hologram. There are also holo-billboards, holo-cameras, holo-letters, holo-journals, holo-cards, holo-communications, holo-flyers, holo-texts, holo-videos, and holo-pictures. Anything that would be made of paper on Wishworld is a hologram on Starland.

Holo–phone: A Starland game much like the Wishworld "Telephone" where a phrase is passed on from one Starling to another and the last Starling says it out loud. The final message is often markedly different from the initial one, much to everyone's amusement.

Hydrong: The equivalent of a Wishworld hundred.

Impossible Wish Orbs: Orbs that are the result of wishes made on Wishworld that are beyond the power of Starlings to grant.

Jujufruit: A large purple fruit with thick skin and juicy flesh. It is bouncy and sometimes used as a ball before being peeled and eaten.

Kaleidoscope City: Where Vega is from. Its colorful downtown is a tourist destination. A factory town, it is well-known for its metal production. Its motto is "If it's made right, it's made in Kaleidoscope City."

Lallabelles: Tiny turqoiuse flowers that grow in clusters. They do not fade and are often used in dried flower arrangements.

Lightning Lounge: The place where students relax and socialize.

Little Dipper Dormitory: Where first- and second-year students live.

Mirror Mantra: A saying specific to each Star Darling that when recited gives her (and her Wisher) reassurance and strength. When a Starling recites her Mirror Mantra while looking in a mirror, she will see her true appearance reflected.

Mooncheese: A mild, tasty cheese often melted in sandwiches, it is made from the milk of the moonnut tree.

Moonfeather: A common material used for stuffing pillows, coats, and toys, moonfeathers are harvested from the moon-feather bush.

Moonium: An amount similar to a Wishworld million.

Moonmoth: Large glowing creatures attracted to light like Wishworld moths.

Moonshot: A very slight possibility.

Noddlenoodle: An extremely long, thin noodle often used in Starling soups, one single noodle can fill an entire bowl.

Ozziefruit: Sweet plum-sized indigo fruit that grows on pink-leaved trees. It is usually eaten raw, made into jam, or cooked into pies. Starling Academy has an ozziefruit orchard.

Queezle: Vega's Power Crystal. Sparkling crystalline blue nuggets held together by their own internal magnetic force. Their seemingly chaotic arrangement actually represents a precise mathematical equation.

Roxylinda: A coral-colored flower with a large blossom.

Safety starglasses: Worn by Starlings to protect their eyes when close to a shooting star.

Serenity Gardens: Extensive botanical gardens set on an island in Luminous Lake.

Shimmering Shores: The sparkly beach located on the banks of Luminous Lake.

Shooting stars: Speeding stars that Starlings can latch on to and ride to Wishworld.

Solar metal: A common, inexpensive kind of metal.

Sparkle Meal: A premade meal.

Sparkle O's: A sweet, fruity cereal, not usually considered a healthy breakfast.

Spill the stars: To tell someone everything.

Starcake: A Starling breakfast item, similar to a star-shaped Wishworld pancake.

Star Caves: The caverns underneath Starling Academy where the Star Darlings' secret Wish-Cavern is located.

Starf!: A Starling expression of dismay.

Star flash: News bulletin, often used starcastically.

Starland: The irregularly shaped world where Starlings live. It is veiled by a bright yellow glow that from a distance makes it look like a star.

Starlight: An expression used to mean public attention. When all eyes are on a Starling, she is said to be "in the starlight."

Starling Academy: The most prestigious all-girl four-year boarding school for wish granting on Starland.

Starlings: The glowing beings with sparkly skin that live on Starland.

Starmin: Sixty starsecs (or seconds) on Starland; the equivalent of a Wishworld minute.

Starriest: As in "I don't have the starriest idea." Used to express lack of knowledge or understanding.

Star salutations: A Starling expression of thanks.

Starsec: A brief period of time, similar to a Wishworld second.

Star Wranglers: Starlings whose job is to lasso a shooting star, to transport Starlings to Wishworld.

Star-Zap: The ultimate smartphone that Starlings use for all communications. It has myriad features.

Stellation: Point of a star. Halo Hall has five stellations, each housing a different department.

Toothlight: A high-tech gadget that Starlings use to clean their teeth.

Violina: A pale blue cone-shaped flower with clusters of shiny, dark blue leaves.

Wharfle: A round metal disk used for Winkedly Wharfles, a game similar to tiddlywinks where you flick disks into a container.

Wish Blossom: The bloom that appears from a Wish Orb after its wish is granted.

Wish energy: The positive energy that is released when a wish is granted. Wish energy powers everything on Starland.

Wish energy manipulation: The ability to mentally harness wish energy to perform physical acts, like turning off lights, closing doors, etc.

Wisher: The Wishling who has made the wish that is being granted.

Wish-House: The place where Wish Orbs are planted and cared for until they sparkle.

Wishlings: The inhabitants of Wishworld.

Wish Mission: The task a Starling undertakes when she travels to Wishworld to help grant a wish.

Wish Orb: The form a wish takes on Wishworld before traveling to Starland. It will grow and sparkle when it's time to grant the wish.

Wish Pendant: A gadget that absorbs and transports wish energy, helps Starlings locate their Wishers, and changes a Starling's appearance. Each Wish Pendant holds a different special power for its Star Darling.

Wish-Watcher: A Starling whose job is to observe the Good Wish Orbs until they glow, indicating that they are ready to be granted.

Wishworld: The planet Starland relies on for wish energy. The beings on Wishworld know it by another name—Earth.

Wishworld Outfit Selector: A program on each Star-Zap that accesses Wishworld fashions for Starlings to wear to blend in.

Wishworld Surveillance Deck: Located high above the campus, it is where Starling Academy students go to observe Wishlings through high-powered telescopes.

Zeldabloom: Large, fragrant purple flowers with yellow centers.

Zing: A traditional Starling breakfast drink. It can be enjoyed hot or iced.

Zoomberries: Small, sweetly tart berries that grow in abundance on Starland.

Acknowledgments

It is impossible to list all of our gratitude, but we will try.

Our most precious gift and greatest teacher, Halo; we love you more than there are stars in the sky . . . punashaku. To the rest of our crazy, awesome, unique tribe—thank you for teaching us to go for our dreams. Integrity. Strength. Love. Foundation. Family. Grateful. Mimi Muldoon—from your star doodling to naming our Star Darlings, your artistry, unconditional love, and inspiration is infinite. Didi Muldoon—your belief and support in us is only matched by your fierce protection and massive-hearted guidance. Gail. Queen G. Your business sense and witchy wisdom are legendary. Frank—you are missed and we know you are watching over us all. Along with Tutu, Nana, and Deda, who are always present, gently guiding us in spirit. To our colorful, totally genius, and bananas siblings—Patrick, Moon, Diva, and Dweezil—there is more creativity and humor in those four names than most people experience in a lifetime. Blessed. To our magical nieces—Mathilda, Zola, Ceylon, and Mia—the Star Darlings adore you and so do we. Our witchy cuzzie fairy godmothers—Ane and Gina. Our fairy fashion godfather, Paris. Our sweet Panay. Teeta and Freddy—we love you all so much. And our four-legged fur babies—Sandwich, Luna, Figgy, and Pinky Star.

The incredible Barry Waldo. Our SD partner. Sent to us from above in perfect timing. Your expertise and friendship are beyond words. We love you and Gary to the moon and back. Long live the manifestation room!

Catherine Daly—the stars shined brightly upon us the day we aligned with you. Your talent and inspiration are otherworldly; our appreciation cannot be expressed in words. Many heartfelt hugs for you and the adorable Oonagh.

To our beloved Disney family. Thank you for believing in us. Wendy Lefkon, our master guide and friend through this entire journey. Stephanie Lurie, for being the first to believe in Star Darlings. Suzanne Murphy, who helped every step of the way. Jeanne Mosure, we fell in love with you the first time we met, and Star Darlings wouldn't be what it is without you. Andrew Sugerman, thank you so much for all your support.

Our team . . . Devon (pony pants) and our Monsterfoot crew—so grateful. Richard Scheltinga—our angel and protector. Chris Abramson—thank you! Special appreciation to Richard Thompson, John LaViolette, Swanna, Mario, and Sam.

To our friends old and new—we are so grateful to be on this rad journey that is life with you all. Fay. Jorja. Chandra. Sananda. Sandy. Kathryn. Louise. What wisdom and strength you share. Ruth, Mike, and the rest of our magical Wagon Wheel bunch—how lucky we are. How inspiring you are. We love you.

Last—we have immeasurable gratitude for every person we've met along our journey, for all the good and the bad; it is all a gift. From the bottom of our hearts we thank you for touching our lives.

Shana Muldoon Zappa is a jewelry designer and writer who was born and raised in Los Angeles. She has an endless imagination and a passion to inspire positivity through her many artistic endeavors. She and her husband, Ahmet Zappa, collaborated on Star Darlings especially for their magical little girl and biggest inspiration, Halo Violetta Zappa.

Ahmet Zappa is the *New York Times* best-selling author of *Because I'm Your Dad* and *The Monstrous Memoirs of a Mighty McFearless*. He writes and produces films and television shows and loves pancakes, unicorns, and making funny faces for Halo and Shana.

Scarlet Discovers True Strength

"Hellooooo?"

Scarlet turned from the window at the sound of a reedy, shrill voice calling from below. She slid from the window seat and peered down the stairs. "Who's there?" she said cautiously, not sure she wanted to know.

As she started down the curving ladder, a Starling came into view. It was a woman—an old woman, Scarlet could tell immediately—grinning and bent over a crystal-tipped cane.

"Hello?" Scarlet said. Her eyes swept the room uneasily for a glimpse of her roommate, Mira. "Er, excuse me," she said, not finding her, "but how did you get in?" Usually, Scarlet was the one sneaking up on people, not the other way around. Plus, as far as she knew, the only way to open the door was by using the palm scanner outside. Then it had to approve you. So how did she get in? "Er . . . can I help you?"

The little old Starling craned her neck to peer up at Scarlet. "Why, hello, and star salutations, dearie," she said sweetly. Her voice cracked with age. Wire-rimmed star-shaped glasses rested halfway down her nose, and silvery lilac curls framed her pinched but pleasant face. "As a matter of fact, you can. I'm looking for my granddaughter, Mira. The Bot-Bot guard at the front told me this was her room?"

"Oh . . ." That made a little more sense. Scarlet guessed family members' hands must work on the palm scanners, too. Not that she would know. After two and a half staryears at Starling Academy, her own family had still never visited her, not once. The only time Scarlet saw her parents was when she met them on tour. They were classical musicians and composers, famous for their otherworldly sounds and scores. Scarlet's mother played the halo-harp, her father the violin, and they traveled staryear-round throughout Starland, recording holo-albums and selling out prestigious concert halls. Even when they played in Starland City, Starland's capital and the home of Starling Academy, rehearsals and interviews kept them so busy that Scarlet always had to go to them. Their schedules were simply too full to fit in a visit to the school.

Growing up, Scarlet had toured Starland with her parents, living out of suitcases, staying in five-star hotels. In between shows, her mother or father—depending on whose turn it was—would tutor her backstage as they tuned their precious instruments. By the time she had reached the Age of Fulfillment, Scarlet had met every dignitary on Starland—but not many other kids.

Scarlet's parents were naturally proud and not in the least surprised when she showed an interest in music early on. They were astonished, however, when she chose to play the *drums* and began to wear a lot of black. At first, she'd just wanted to shock and annoy them and rebel against their stodgy, stuffy ways. And she succeeded in this—particularly when she started adding thick black streaks to her hot-pink hair. Soon, though, she found herself loving the drums and her adopted color, too. Both made her feel independent and strong. Both let her show her feelings without having to say a single word.

Still, Scarlet needed more. She needed a life that was

truly her own, which was why she had applied to Starling Academy. She was stunned when she got in and sure she would struggle in her classes, but she found they were easy for her. The only things that were hard were fitting in and making friends.

"What's the matter, dearie?" The elder Starling chuckled. "Black hole got your tongue?"

"Oh . . . star apologies," Scarlet said quickly. She was suddenly aware that she probably seemed rude. "Uh, yes. Yes, this is Mira's room. But, well . . ." She looked around and shrugged. "She's not here."

"Oh, what a pity!" The woman's face folded into a pained expression, like one of those comedy/tragedy masks that hung over Mira's bed. She sighed and shook her head slowly. "Well. I suppose I'll just wait for her, then. I should have told her I was coming. Hopefully she won't be long." She shuffled across the room, smiling sweetly and looking ever so slightly confused. "Please do forgive me for surprising you. I didn't realize she had a roommate, you see. I could have sworn the last time she wrote to me she said she lived alone."

"She did," said Scarlet. "I just moved in." She tried, with little success, she knew, to sound less bitter than she felt.

"Ah, good!" said the old woman. "Glad to know I wasn't wrong." She tapped her head just above her ear. "Two thousand and three and still sharp as a prism. So what's your name, my dear?"

"It's, um, Scarlet."

"Scarlet! How lovely! We had a glowsow on the farm with that name when I was a girl. Stubborn as a glow-fur, if I remember . . . ah, but aren't they all? So!" She crossed the star-trimmed corners of her gauzy, glittering crocheted shawl. "Just moved in, you say. Does that mean you're new?"

"No, ma'am . . ." Scarlet shook her head and turned back to her loft, longing to climb back up. She was usually so glad her new roommate, Mira, was always at "play rehearsal," or whatever that drama stuff she loved so much was. For once, though, Scarlet wished she would hurry back to their room so her grandmother would have someone else to talk to.

The old woman, meanwhile, settled onto the bench in front of Mira's dressing table with a frail yet eager sigh. She took a moment to catch her breath and take in Scarlet's side of the wide, softly lit room. Her eyes lingered on the hot-pink drum set perched on a raised platform across from Scarlet's black-and-fuschia-covered bed. Scarlet's things had been moved for her the same starday Lady Stella had broken the news. When her Star-Zap finally led her to her newly assigned room on the other side of the Big Dipper Dorm, it wasn't clear who was more put out: Mira, who'd been quite content having a single, or Scarlet herself.

"Are those drums?" asked the old woman, pointing.

Scarlet nodded. What else would they be?

"Ooh! What fun! Can I try them?" She was already out of her seat. She hobbled over to the platform, raised her cane, and gave the cymbal a surprisingly powerful smack.

CRASHHH!

"Don't! *Stop!*" Scarlet cried, hurrying over. "I mean, I'd rather you didn't, um, please." Scarlet didn't want to be rude, but nobody—not even a little old Starling—was touching her precious drums. "Maybe you'd be more comfortable waiting for Mira in the Luminous Library. I'm sure a Bot-Bot guide could show you the way."

"Oh, starry nights, no." The old woman grinned and set her cane back on the polished star-studded floor. "I'm just as comfortable as can be. Where is my lovely grand-daughter, though, do you know? I'm just as eager to see her as I can be."

Scarlet didn't know, though she wanted to be help-ful. If Mira had ever said anything to her about where she was going, Scarlet was too focused on her Star Dar-lings problem to care. Besides, Scarlet preferred for other Starlings to keep their noses out of her business, so she tried to set an example by keeping her nose to her-self, too.

"I'm not sure . . . maybe play rehearsal?"

"Oh, yes, you're right, I'm sure!" crowed the old woman. "That Mira is quite an actor! Destined for star-dom! Don't you think?"

"Is she? I don't know," Scarlet confessed. "I've never seen her act." Since leaving her parents to attend Starling Academy, she'd tried to steer clear of theaters and audi-toriums. Quite frankly, she also had yet to see the appeal in running around, dressed up like a fool, pretending to be somebody else.

"Moon and stars!" Mira's grandmother gasped. "Never? What a shame. Oh, but surely you've seen her act *sometime*. . . ."

Scarlet shook her head. "Star apologies. No."

"Never?" The old woman leaned forward, twisting slightly. The corners of her mouth twitched, one at a time. A bluish star-shaped freckle on her cheek began to sparkle. Scarlet watched it closely, the familiarity clicking at last. How hadn't she noticed it before?

"All right, I'll admit it." Scarlet sighed to hold back a groan. "I saw her once."

"Really? You did see her? When?"

"The Time of Shadows production. Our first year at school."

"Oh, that was a good one!"

Scarlet stifled a smile as she clicked her tongue and slowly shook her head.

"It wasn't?" The woman's blue eyes grew round. "You really don't think so? Why not?"

"Well, some parts were good . . . like the scenery. . . . And the props could have been worse."

"What about the acting?" croaked the old woman.

Scarlet looked down and smiled.

"*Well?*" Mira's "grandmother" waited, tapping her cane against the floor, sending sparks into the air. "Wasn't it good? Of course it was! We got a standing ovation at the end!"

"*We?*" Scarlet glanced back up, raising one eyebrow in a sharp arch.

The old woman threw back her head. "*Starf!* You knew it was me!" she groaned. Then she laughed and tossed off her shawl so it dangled behind her. "Tell me I had you going there for a while, though," Mira said as she pulled off her wig. Her long indigo hair spilled down her back in shimmering waves. Beneath a thick layer of stage makeup, a whole galaxy of bright blue freckles flashed like sunlight on a lake.

"For a starmin," muttered Scarlet. She did have to live with her, after all.

"Really? Is that all?" Mira sighed. "Sunspots. I guess that's why you're not in that remedial group anymore." She grinned at Scarlet—then blanched in the heat of Scarlet's simmering glare. "No offense!" she said quickly. Like everyone at Starling Academy, it seemed, Mira assumed the special class the Star Darlings went to last period was for extra help so they didn't fail out of school. "Star apologies. I just thought . . . you know . . . since it was a mistake and all . . ."

"It was a mistake, all right," hissed Scarlet.

"Are you mad?"

Am I mad? thought Scarlet. Did a glowfur eat green globules? She was mad, all right. Madder than Leona when she'd had to try out for her own band!

Suddenly, Scarlet's Star-Zap beeped. A holo-text was coming in.

She read it: IN THE HEDGE MAZE. R U STILL COMING?

It was Vega, waiting to meet.

"Forget about it. I'll be fine," Scarlet snapped as she climbed off her bed.

She'd be perfectly *startacular* . . . just as soon as she set everything straight again.